SIGNED +

ALL THE LONELY PEOPLE

**This special signed hardcover edition
is limited to 300 copies.**

This is number:

296

David B. Silva

Mike Bohatch

ALL THE LONELY PEOPLE

David B. Silva

FIRST EDITION

All the Lonely People © 2003 by David B. Silva
Cover Artwork & Foil Design © 2003 by Mike Bohatch
All Rights Reserved.

This book is a work of fiction. Names, characters, places and incidents are either a product of the author's imagination or are used fictitiously. Any resemblance to actual events, locales or persons, living or dead, is entirely coincidental.

DELIRIUM BOOKS
P.O. Box 338
North Webster, IN 46555
srstaley@deliriumbooks.com
http://www.deliriumbooks.com

For more information on this book or other titles, please visit the Delirium Books' official website at: http://www.deliriumbooks.com.

This book is offered as a limited edition of 300 signed and numbered hardcovers (ISBN 1-929653-57-3; $45.00) and a 26-copy deluxe, slipcased leatherbound edition ($175.00).

ACKNOWLEDGEMENTS

I always try to put a book together on my own, at least as much as possible. Not because I don't want (or often, need) help, but because I hate to inconvenience people with my nagging questions. I wasn't able to get away with it this time. So let me extend my appreciation to Dan Titus for putting up with my questions and helping me to understand an environment of which I had very little knowledge.

A special thanks as well to Kealan Patrick Burke for keeping me honest.

—DBS

1

When the old man came through the front door, Chase Hanford glanced up from his newspaper and didn't think much about it. This was a face he hadn't seen before, and though that was unusual for a bar like The Last Stop, it wasn't unheard of.

A little dive, set off Old Coyote Road on the outskirts of town, with sawdust on the floor and pine paneling on the walls, The Last Stop was like the jukebox next to the front door. It didn't get much play, but it had its regulars. They straggled in nearly every night, usually under the cover of darkness because it was easier to drink alone when you sat in the shadows.

Chase took the lean off the back legs of his stool and stood up.

The old man wiped his feet on the mat just inside the door. He turned his collar down. It was the middle of winter, cold enough outside to burn your lungs if you took too deep a breath. He nodded, friendly enough. Cradled in one arm, he held a small carton. Nothing fancy. Made of cardboard, it appeared. Something large enough to hold a book or two, if that were the sort of thing you liked to carry around with you.

The stranger sat down on the bar stool closest to the door, and placed the carton on the counter.

"What can I get you?" Chase asked.

David B. Silva / 7

"A draft would be fine." He peeled off his gloves and overcoat, while Chase drew his beer. He appeared to be in his mid-to-late sixties. No color in his face. Clean shaven. Short-cropped hair that had been longer before a recent cut. You could tell by the band of white skin that started behind his ears and dipped beneath the collar of his suit jacket.

Chase placed the mug on the counter, along with a napkin and a bowl of peanuts.

The stranger blew into his cupped hands, rubbed them together, then fished his wallet out of the inside pocket of his jacket. He tipped Chase an extra buck. Nobody tipped in these parts. You might get some lucky bastard who'd won a few bucks on a football pool or down at the Indian casino who'd buy a round for everyone, but no one tipped. Just didn't happen. This guy wasn't a local. He was passing through on his way down to the Bay Area or maybe north to Portland or Seattle.

"Thanks," Chase said, snapping the bills.

The stranger nodded, once again friendly enough. Then he gave some serious consideration to his beer before finally taking a sip. Chase had seen that same look before. It usually belonged to someone with a drinking problem, someone who wasn't sure if he wanted to start down that road again or not. That may or may not have been the case this time out. There was no way to know for certain.

The stranger lowered his head, one hand attending to the cardboard box. He didn't look up again for a good long time, and he didn't offer anything along the lines of conversation.

Chase went back to his newspaper.

All the Lonely People / 8

2

Ben Tucker, decked out in that same camouflage hunting jacket he always wore (even though he hadn't gone after a buck in better than ten years), came through the door a few minutes later. He was strictly a Moosehead man. Chase let him run a tab somewhere around a hundred bucks, which was better than three times what he usually let a customer carry. The thing was, Ben had been coming in since day one, and Chase knew if pressed the man would take care of the tab on the spot. Besides, Ben had had a string of bad luck lately. He'd lost his wife late last year, after to a long bout with stomach cancer, and the illness had taken nearly as much out of Ben's guts as it had out of his wife's.

"Hey," Chase said, pulling a bottle out of the refrigerator and popping the cap before Ben even bothered asking. "Cold out there?"

"Warm if you're a penguin." Ben scooped up the Moosehead and settled into his favorite booth, directly across from the counter. "Damn cold for the rest of us."

Chase grinned and checked with the stranger. "Like me to add a little foam to that?"

He shook his head, placed his hand over the mouth of the mug.

"Let me know if you change your mind."

"I will."

Ben raised an eyebrow and nodded curiously in the stranger's direction. It wasn't often you came across a complete stranger in a place like The Last Stop. When you did, he tended to stick out like a hundred dollar bill in the church offering. Maybe this man more than most, since he was hunched over his drink like he was worried someone might try to steal it from him. And then there was that cardboard box he'd brought in with him. It didn't look like much, but there had to be something to it. Otherwise, why would he bother hauling it around?

Chase shrugged silently. He didn't know what to make of the man, either. He'd been robbed once, the first year he owned the place. Just before closing, a young kid around nineteen or twenty put the barrel of a 12 gauge in his face and told him to empty the register. Chase had done as he was asked—he liked to say he wasn't the smartest man you'd ever meet but he wasn't a fool, either—and the kid made off with three hundred and ninety-four dollars. They caught him the next day, sticking that same barrel into some other bartender's face, only the second guy was smart enough to have a .44 under the counter. The point being . . . it only took once. After that Chase had always kept a close eye when a stranger came into The Last Stop.

Maddie Ashburn, who would dance naked on the counter for a free beer if that was the kind of place Chase wanted to run, straggled in next. She was followed by Sam Morgan and Charlie Wood, and gradually the place began to fill up with the kind of background chatter that was easy to tune out because you were so used to it.

The first person to ask about the stranger was Herb Canfield. Herb was a hardcore *Cheers* fan. He looked a little like Norm Peterson. Round-faced. Heavyset. Clothes always a little sloppy. Liked to sit at the bar, near the back. And whenever he got the chance, he liked to use lines he'd picked up from *Cheers*.

"What would you like, Herb?"

"A reason to live," he'd say. "Give me a beer."

All the Lonely People / 10

"How's life treating you, Herb?"

"Like it caught me with its wife," he'd say.

Sometimes he'd slip one by that Chase hadn't heard before, but most of them made the rounds more than once. In his heart of hearts Herb probably was Norm, a man who liked his routine, who didn't mind poking a little fun at himself. There were a lot of Norms that came and went at The Last Stop. Herb was just the one that seemed to stick out.

Chase placed a Red Dog on the counter in front of him. "That keep you?"

"Until the dog stops biting," he said with a grin. He nodded at the old man at the other end. "So who's the stranger? Looks like he's carrying the world on his shoulders."

"Don't know," Chase said. He'd had customers come in, order a beer, take a sip or two and leave, that happened more often than you'd imagine, but he'd never had someone nurse a beer all night like they did on TV or in the movies. This guy looked like he might stretch that beer over the next week or two at the rate he was going. Something was on his mind, 'cause his thoughts sure as hell weren't on drinking. "Came in about half-an-hour ago. Still working on his first beer."

"Just passing through?"

"I suppose."

Herb took a sip of his Red Dog, and peered past the bottle. "What's with the box?"

"Your guess is as good as mine," Chase said with a shrug. He wiped down the counter, mostly making busy work for himself, then gradually wandered down to the other end. "Still no foam on that?"

"I'm fine, thanks."

"Not often we get an unfamiliar face in here."

"I'm surprised," he said. "Nice place you have."

"Kind of you to say," Chase said with a faint nod. Behind that nod, the thought went through his head: *You can't believe what he tells you, Chase. Not a word. Not*

David B. Silva / 11

from a man who will look you in the eye and tell you The Last Stop is a nice place. It wasn't that the bar was a dump; it wasn't. But it wasn't anything to remark about, either. There was an old saying that the words of a drunk were the thoughts of a sober man, and in Chase's experience that was truer than not. But that didn't mean the words were always honest. When a guy wanders in, fiddles with his drink, then tells you something you know isn't the God's honest truth, a flag goes up. Maybe he was just being polite. Or maybe it would be smart not to take anything that came out of his mouth too seriously.

"Hey! You gonna lollygag all night back there, pretending like you're actually doing something, or you gonna get me another beer?" Ben said heartily.

Chase grinned at the stranger, rapped the back of his knuckles on the counter in a friendly enough gesture, and turned his attention to his regular customer. "That's a Shirley Temple, right Ben?"

"Right. Just add a little Moosehead, will ya?"

"You got it." Chase pulled out a Moosehead, popped the cap and carried it around the counter to the booth where Ben was sitting across from Sam. He placed the bottle on the table.

"Sit for a sec," Sam said, eyeing the stranger.

Chase sat down. "I don't know who he is, and I don't know what's in the box."

"Probably hawking encyclopedias," Ben said.

Maddie, who was sitting in the adjacent booth, raised up slightly. "Or Girl Scout cookies."

"I don't think he's a salesman," Chase said.

"Then what about the box?"

"What about it? For all we know it's his dead mother's ashes."

"Ask him," Maddie said.

"You ask him." Chase started to get up, but Sam pulled him down again.

"What's the harm?"

"For one thing, it's none of our damn business."

***All the Lonely People* / 12**

Chase said this quietly, fully aware the conversation had disintegrated into the kind of whispering you heard in junior high cafeterias, with one group of kids giggling and glancing nervously over their shoulders at another. "Besides, he's a customer. He has a right to drink his beer in peace."

"It's a harmless little question," Maddie said.

"It's none of our business."

The stranger looked up from his drink, his eyes bright and curious. "I'm sorry. Is there some sort of a problem?"

"No," Chase said apologetically. He slid out of the booth. "No problem."

"Go ahead." Maddie motioned to the old man. "Ask him."

"Ask me what?"

"It's nothing," Chase said. "I'm sorry for the bother."

"The cardboard box," Sam said. "We're curious about it."

"The box is just a box. It's what's inside that you might find interesting." The stranger grinned engagingly, and Chase didn't know about the others, but he didn't like the way that grin looked on the stranger's face. It looked as if there were something hidden behind it, something not quite so endearing. "It's something I picked up at a yard sale in a little town south of Weed. A woman sold it to me. She said she found it at the bottom of a trunk that belonged to her grandmother. She'd never noticed it before. Not in the trunk. Not in any of her grandmother's belongings. But there it was."

The stranger pushed his beer to one side, and moved the cardboard carton across the counter to take its place. He looked down upon it as if he were a magician gazing down upon a woman he was about to saw in half. "I asked her if she was sure she wanted to sell it, since it had belonged to her grandmother. I know my wife holds onto family heirlooms as if they were all she had left in the world. This woman . . . she said she wasn't sure it really

David B. Silva / 13

belonged to her grandmother—wasn't sure who it belonged to—but she was sure she didn't want it in the house."

"I asked her why," the man added. "She said it was because it gave her the willies."

Ben and Sam climbed out of the booth and quietly drifted across the room. When Chase, who was back behind the counter, became aware of them, they were standing on either side of the man, staring down at the box as if it held the secret of life.

"So what's in it?" Ben asked.

Chase found himself silently asking the same question Ben had asked: What's in it?

"It's called a spirit box," the stranger said. The old man pulled back the cardboard flaps, reached in, and brought out a small, rectangular box made of rosewood. He placed the box on the counter, where the overhead fluorescents reflected dully off a symbol carved in the wood. The symbol, a circle inside a circle inside a crescent, vaguely resembled the eye on the back of the one dollar bill, just above the pyramid. Chase could understand why the woman had wanted to get rid of it. There was something immediately creepy about it.

"I bought it for my wife," the man said. "Couldn't help myself."

He ran his hand across the top, which showed wear around the edges where the finish was faded and scarred. "She hasn't been well in quite some time. Hormones. Depression. I'm sure you understand. Perhaps if I didn't travel so much in my work . . ."

"What do you do?" Sam asked.

"I'm a collector of sorts. Always in search of the rare and undervalued."

"Uh-huh," Ben said. "So what's the story with the box?"

"You see this symbol here on the lid? Looks like an eye? That's a Yaqui Indian hieroglyphic." Nervously, with fingers that trembled, the man toyed with the lid.

All the Lonely People / 14

One side lifted slightly and Chase thought he saw a sliver of bright light escape before the lid dropped back into place. "A warning of sorts, you might say. Traditionally, the box was given as a gift to an enemy. It was used to capture his spirit."

"How come you know so much about this stuff?"

"Just a hobby," the man said. "Something I've studied a bit."

"You open it yet?" Ben asked.

"Haven't had the nerve."

"Maybe we should leave it at that?" Chase suggested. He toweled off a shot glass, making busy work for himself, feeling increasingly uneasy without knowing why.

The man nodded. "That might be best."

"You're kidding, right?" Sam moved the cardboard container off the counter, onto a nearby stool, and pressed in closer. "You've got it out. Might as well give us a look-see."

"Only seems fair," Ben said.

The stranger looked across the counter at Chase for permission, only Chase found himself drifting back to an earlier thought: *You can't trust what he tells you. Not a word.* "Maybe another time."

"He's just passing through," Sam said, patting the stranger on the shoulder. "That's right, ain't it? You're just passing through?"

"On my way back home," he said.

"See? We don't get a look now, we're never gonna get a look."

"Some things are better left unseen," Chase said.

"What the hell's that supposed to mean?"

He didn't know how to explain it. All he knew was that he wasn't nearly as interested in seeing what the box held as he was in seeing the man carry it back out the door. "You losers want to look in the box, look in the damn box. You don't need my permission."

Sam gave the stranger another pat on the shoulder, offering his own permission.

David B. Silva / 15

"You sure?" the old man asked. He sounded as if it were all settled, the way your conscience sounds when you've already decided on that second slice of pie that you know you don't need. "I can box it back up."

"Just open the damn thing and get it over with," Sam said.

"As long as you're sure."

Maddie was up out of her booth now. James Cleaver, who worked over at Evanhoe, Matson & Company as a junior accountant (a numbers man, who liked things lined up in straight columns so he could make sense of them), crowded in next to her, as nearly everyone else in the place began to gather around. All of them curious. All of them on their toes and leaning in to get a better look.

Chase had no intention of joining the crowd. He trusted his gut enough to know a bad feeling when it stirred. He went to add the clean shot glass to the stack behind the bar, and while his back was turned, the stranger raised the lid on the rosewood box.

Out of the corner of his eye, Chase caught an explosion of blinding light.

And the color bled instantly out of the room, turning everything gray, then white.

All the Lonely People / 16

PART II:
I AM A TOWN

1

Time stood still.

Color bleached from the bottles behind the bar, from the pine wood paneling, the rainbow-colored glass in the jukebox. Every person, every mug, stool, table, all of them faded into the blinding void.

Searing pain burrowed deep behind Chase's eyes.

His hands went to his face.

The breath went out of him, as if someone had buried a fist in his gut. His knees buckled. He collapsed to the floor.

Twenty seconds passed. Maybe thirty. Maybe longer.

Gradually, Chase became aware of the bottles clanging on the shelves behind him. The pain at the back of his eyes began to recede. With a great deal of effort, he climbed back to his feet.

He wasn't sure how much time had actually passed, but he knew it had been longer than it seemed. His entire life had passed before his eyes. At age six, the potholder he made out of yarn for Mother's Day. At age ten when he conned his sister into washing the dishes for him. The time he stole a pocketful of jawbreakers from the corner grocery. The first time he kissed his wife. The birth of his daughter. It was all there. Every hour. Every minute. Every second of his life.

Chase blinked and felt warm tears run down his cheeks.

The blinding absence of color began to subside. Even while there was still pain in his eyes, he was slowly able to make out the general shape of the old boat oar tacked to the back wall. The green tint of the light shade hanging over the table nearest the men's room came into focus next. Followed by the first dollar bill he'd ever made at The Last Stop, which was framed and hung on the wall to his right, next to his business license.

Nearby, Sam was glassy-eyed and unsteady. An odd smile masked his face, as if he'd been struck in the head and was suffering the aftereffects. He blinked a few times, rubbed at his eyes. He kept one hand braced against the counter for support.

"You okay?" Chase asked.

He nodded weakly.

Next to him, Ben plopped down on a stool and held his head in both hands, the way he did sometimes when he'd had a few more than he could handle. He closed his eyes. His breathing became deep and laborious.

Chase gave him a nudge. "Ben?"

"Yeah, just give me a minute."

Maddie started toward the front door on legs that didn't look as if they were going to get her there. She stopped at the jukebox, leaned against it with both hands, then fumbled around in her purse until she came up with a quarter. A familiar Mary Chapin Carpenter song came on, something about being a town. Maddie listened to a few lines, then sank to the floor, her face expressionless, empty. She looked like a ghost. Ashen. Nearly transparent.

What was going on?

What had happened to everyone?

"Think I'm gonna go," Sam said, wiping a weathered hand across his mouth. He looked older than his fifty-seven years and Chase wasn't sure if that was because he'd never really given Sam a close look before or if it had something to do with Sam's drinking.

Or maybe something to do with the light.

All the Lonely People / 20

"Maybe that's best," Chase agreed, which struck him as an odd thing to say. It also struck him as odd that he hoped the others would follow Sam out the door. Chase didn't think he'd caught the worst of whatever the hell that light inside the box had held, but he had caught enough,. It had left him feeling numb and in a fog.

"Think I'll be going, too," Ben said. He raised his head off the counter, took a peek under his arm at Sam heading toward the door, and climbed off the stool. He staggered momentarily, fiddling with his camouflage hunting jacket, which had become twisted around his waist. He couldn't look at Chase—or didn't want to, Chase wasn't sure which—and that was all right, because Chase didn't think he could look at Ben, either. Not in the eye.

"Next time," Chase said.

"Yeah. Next time."

Herb Canfield, who had somehow found his way back to the far end of the counter, climbed off his stool and let out a heavy sigh. He stood on wobbly legs a moment, his round Norm Peterson face partially hidden behind one hand, then moved down the line of stools one at a time, using them for balance.

As he reached the end of the bar, he saluted half-heartedly. "Another night, my friend."

"Sure, Herb. Another night."

Chase could barely keep track of his thoughts, which seemed almost dream-like, but he became aware of something missing from this scene. Not just out of place, but actually missing.

The old man.

The rosewood box was gone, too. As was the cardboard box that had held it. And the old man's gloves and overcoat. *Poof!* Like magic. All he had left behind was the barely touched mug of beer, which was still sitting on the counter.

Strange.

Across the room, Maddie managed to climb back to her feet. She leaned against the jukebox, mumbling

David B. Silva / 21

something Chase couldn't make out. Her next step sent her stumbling into the door. A gust of cold air scurried in as it opened, then found cover at the back of the bar as Maddie disappeared into the winter night and the door closed again.

Chase closed his eyes.

The pain rattling around inside his head eased momentarily, then stirred again, worse this time.

He leaned against the shelf of liquor bottles, the chime of bottles sounding miles away. Every muscle in his body felt weak and weary.

Scary, isn't it?

The thought flowed through him like a cold wave.

Scary how easy it is to start adding groups to the list.

Chase opened his eyes.

James Cleaver was the last remaining customer. He stood motionless at the end of the bar, his eyes glassy, until a shudder went through his body and he seemed to return to the moment. He smiled crookedly. "Something doesn't feel right. I think I better call it a night."

Chase nodded.

Cleaver pushed away from the bar and started toward the door, walking haltingly, dragging the tips of his shoes across the floor then turning them up just before his foot came down with each step. Even though it wasn't true, he looked like a man who'd had way too much to drink. He bounced off the door jamb with his left shoulder, backed up seemingly in a daze, then tried again and disappeared out the door.

Chase leaned forward against the counter, dropping his head between his arms and staring at the rubber mat on the floor. Remnants of white clouded the outer edges of his vision. He took a deep breath that felt as if it had nowhere to go, let it out slowly, and decided James Cleaver had been right. Something didn't feel right.

The song on the jukebox ended.

Chase raised his head and suddenly felt like a man who had just come out of an eye exam with dilated pupils.

All the Lonely People / **22**

He shaded his eyes against the bright lights, the pain at the back of his eyes throbbing dully.

There was a dimmer switch next to the door to the office. He turned it down until he could see again without the pain. Then he leaned against the wall and gazed out over the empty room.

What had happened here?

What the hell had happened?

2

It was one o'clock in the morning, a couple hours earlier than he usually made it home, and Chase felt something like an intruder as he entered the house.

He came in through the laundry room, doing his best to keep quiet, making his way through the darkness with relative ease. He dropped his keys on the counter, emptied his pocket change into a tray, and plugged the cell phone into its battery charger. This was the same routine he went through every night, but this time it didn't feel the same. It felt almost dreamlike.

Without thinking, he flipped on the overhead fluorescent lights in the kitchen and immediately recoiled from the brightness. One hand went to his eyes, the other fumbled for the switch.

The fluorescents went off again. Chase sank to the floor, feeling a searing pain burrow deep into his head, and wondered how long this aversion to light was going to continue.

It had already gone on too long.

It took awhile before he moved from the floor. He waited until most of the pain had passed. Then he dragged himself back to his feet and went out to the garage, where he got a pair of sunglasses out of the glove compartment of the car.

When he returned, he used the recessed accent lights

All the Lonely People / 24

under the cabinets instead of the overhead fluorescents. They were still bright enough, even with the sunglasses, to cause some discomfort, but it was manageable and he was able to finish making a ham-and-cheese sandwich without too much difficulty.

Unfortunately, by the time he sat down, the sandwich no longer held much appeal. He took a single bite and forced it down for principle's sake. The rest, he covered in plastic wrap and buried on the bottom shelf of the refrigerator, behind a jar of pickles and a tub of margarine.

It was nearly 1:30 now.

Tired, but not really sleepy, Chase sorted through the mail, found nothing of interest, then went upstairs to look in on his daughter. Danielle's room was the first on the right, the one with the door that was always open in case there was ever a problem.

Almost ten, Danielle had recently started to fuss about her lack of privacy. It hadn't done her any good. The door needed to be open. Simple as that. If she was having problems breathing, they needed to be able to hear. End of discussion.

Chase paused in the doorway, then ventured into the room to stand at his daughter's bedside. She was breathing comfortably, which was always a good sign. They'd been fortunate up to this point. There were the thirty-minute physical therapy sessions three times a day, the special diet considerations, plus the digestive problems and the constant struggle to keep her weight up, but overall, Danielle had been able to lead as normal a life as most girls her age. It was hard to ask anything more under the shadows of something like cystic fibrosis.

Absently, Chase breathed in concert with her, waiting for the rhythm to change or the sound of struggle to make itself evident. After a few minutes, when there were no changes, no struggling, Chase kissed Danielle on the forehead and continued down the hall to the master bedroom.

David B. Silva / 25

Karla was asleep on her side, turned away from the dim light of the shaded lamp she always left on for him. Shadow and light outlined the gentle contours of her body, shifting slightly as she took in each breath then let it out again. She was a tiny woman, under five-three in high heels, which she rarely wore because they played havoc with her back. Trim and fit, always willing to put in the time to stay in shape, no matter how busy her schedule.

Chase kissed her on the forehead.

She stirred and grew a smile without opening her eyes.

He peeled off his shirt and toed his way out of his shoes. His body felt as if every muscle were working against him. It wasn't just his muscles, though. It was a sense that something had shifted, that nothing was quite as solid or as certain as it had been yesterday. Chase couldn't quite put his finger on it, certainly couldn't explain it in any rational terms, but he felt as if he were moving through a foreign land where he definitely didn't belong.

On the edge of the bed, he peeled off his jeans and socks, then climbed under the covers. The light went off. Darkness settled in around him, relieving some of the pain behind his eyes. Chase removed his sunglasses and placed them on the nightstand next to the digital clock.

It was 2:38.

Where had the time gone?

All the Lonely People / 26

PART III: ROUTINE AND EXCEPTION

1

Chase felt a nudge and thought Karla was stirring in the bed next to him. Though he generally fell asleep only a couple of hours before she rose in the morning, he always had a distant awareness when she stirred. Too much stirring and he'd come awake to make sure everything was all right.

But this was different.

There was a strange noise somewhere in the background, a noise he couldn't reconcile with the bedroom surroundings.

Another nudge.

Chase reluctantly opened one eye.

Not Karla, but Danielle. And not the bedroom, either. The reason he hadn't been able to reconcile the background noise was because he was in the living room, sitting in his favorite recliner, with the local news playing on the television. Danielle had a clump of his shirt sleeve in her hand and she was tugging on it.

"What are you doing down here?" she asked. "Didn't you go to bed last night?"

He thought he had gone to bed. He remembered undressing. He remembered sitting on the edge of the bed, and checking the digital clock on the nightstand. It had been two-something, later than he'd imagined. He remembered that, too, but that was the last of what he remembered.

"I had trouble sleeping, honey."

"You going to eat breakfast with us?"

Chase wiped the spittle from the corner of his mouth, where he had apparently been drooling, and sat higher in the chair. "Yeah, sure."

"I'll tell Mom." Danielle went skipping out of the room. She was still in her pajamas and outside it was dark behind the living room curtains, so Chase imagined it must be sometime around six. Certainly not much later. He'd slept for three, three-and-a-half hours.

How many of those three-and-a-half hours had he spent right here in the recliner?

Karla appeared in the doorway, a kitchen towel in her hands, a lock of hair hanging down across her forehead. "Couldn't sleep?"

"Strange night at the bar," Chase said.

"You wearing sunglasses to bed now?"

For a moment, he wasn't sure what she meant. Then his hand went to his face and he realized he must have put the sunglasses back on sometime during the night. "My eyes haven't been doing well in the light. The sunglasses seem to help."

Karla nodded. "Since you're awake, you mind taking care of Danielle while I make breakfast?"

"No, sure. No problem."

"She takes her meds with her meal, so she just needs her CPT."

Danielle came bounding back into the room and jumped onto the couch.

Chase climbed out of the chair and dug a pillow out of the cabinet, next to the shelf of VHS movies, where it was always handy. He tossed it to her. She fluffed it up, doubled it over in her lap, and leaned forward with it tucked under her armpits.

"What do you want to watch?" Chase asked.

"Caillou."

"FOX?"

"PBS."

All the Lonely People / 30

After the physical therapy, Chase sat down with them for breakfast. He wasn't terribly hungry, that single bite from the ham-and-cheese sandwich last night seemed to still be with him. And because three-and-a-half hours just weren't enough, he struggled to keep his eyes open. But he managed to get a few bites down and make it through the meal without dozing off.

After that, there was fifteen minutes of panic and scrambling as the two women got ready to leave. Danielle had just started the newest Harry Potter, something called *The Order of the Phoenix*, so she could hardly wait to get to school and do some reading before class. Karla was in a meltdown, claiming they were already running late when it was only a few minutes after seven. They went out the door with Chase promising he'd clear the table and do the dishes before they returned.

But the moment the door closed, the long night caught up with him. Chase collapsed into the living room recliner, still wearing his sunglasses, and promptly fell back to sleep.

2

He woke up blind.

Not completely blind. He could still make out the nearest corner of the room, but it was little more than a thin gray line and he was blind enough that he wasn't sure he could trust it. There was always something suspect about the dark.

He extended his hands, groping in the murk, and dragged his feet across the floor as he moved guardedly to his right. The floor was hard and unforgiving, the nearest wall somewhere just beyond his reach.

Isn't it odd? How so often we're blind to the world around us?

The reverberation of the words was God-like, pervasive. It resonated off nearby surfaces, circled him, then seemed to circle the room again. It was everywhere and nowhere all at the same time.

Chase froze, his arm extended, his feet unwilling to move.

This is what a deer caught in the headlights feels like, he thought.

After a few moments of his heart pounding to escape his chest, he tried sliding to his right until he found a wall. Something solid. *Thank God.*

It smelled like fresh paint, and there was something comforting in that familiarity, like the smell of clean sheets on the bed.

The wall drew him to a corner, which must have been the thin gray line he had picked out of the darkness. Around the corner, he followed the wall to another corner, and then another, until he had counted four altogether and realized he was back where he had started.

There were no doors.

No windows.

No way out.

Chase raised his head and studied the darkness above him. There had to be a ceiling, didn't there? All rooms had a ceiling. Some were taller than others, but they all had ceilings.

Unless this wasn't a room.

He reached toward the boundless overhead, and found no end to the darkness. It could be a matter of inches. Or maybe a foot or two. Or maybe there was no ceiling here. Maybe it went on forever, or so close to forever it might as well be forever.

"Can anybody hear me?"

An echo.

Can anybody hear me?

What did an echo mean? There had to be an end, a surface that had reflected the sound back to him. A ceiling.

"Anyone!"

This brought an echo, too.

Anyone!

But it also brought something else. The floor had begun to rumble.

Nearly knocked off his feet, Chase reached for the support of the wall, grasping for a handle that wasn't there. He jammed two fingers on his right hand, groaned, and suddenly found himself sitting on the floor after his feet had gone out from under him.

It wasn't just the floor that was rumbling, he realized. It was the entire room.

He felt himself lifted off the hard surface, then

David B. Silva / 33

dropped again, like a spineless doll. Pain shot up through his tailbone. He braced himself against the floor, then rolled into the nearest wall and soared into the air again.

When he slammed back to earth, the air emptied out of his lungs.

Thousands of stars began to dance across his vision. Numb and in shock, he gazed mindlessly at the boundless overhead.

Then the first ray of light seemed to open in the sky above him. It felt like the sun coming out after a tornado. A crack split open the darkness, and the opening grew until the light became blinding.

Chase shaded his eyes.

Above him, the old man's face appeared in the sky. He grinned. "What do you think of the box? You like it?"

When he reached down to pick Chase up, Chase came awake in a sweat.

3

Chase drifted in and out of sleep most of the day, and was grateful the dream never returned.

In the early afternoon, Karla called during her lunch break. She reminded him that Danielle had a dentist's appointment after school, so they'd be getting home late and would probably miss him before he went to open the bar. Chase didn't remember anything about the dentist appointment, but assured her he hadn't forgotten and told her he'd be sure to give her a kiss on the forehead when he got home.

"A kiss on the lips would be better," Karla said softly.

"You won't mind if I wake you?"

"Did Snow White mind?"

"I think she was a little crabby afterwards," Chase said.

"I'll make it memorable."

"How could I say no to that?"

There was a moment of silence, Karla's tone shifted, and suddenly a note of concern entered her voice. "You feeling better? You looked . . . a little ragged this morning."

This was the real reason she had called. Not about Danielle's appointment, but because she was worried that something was wrong. And she was right. Something was wrong. Chase just wasn't sure what it was.

David B. Silva / 35

He took in a full breath and came *this* close to telling her about the old man and what had happened in the bar last night. But it would have been a long story and he wasn't sure he even understood what had happened, so he let the temptation pass.

"It was a long night. That's all. I'll be fine."

"You aren't planning on sleeping in the chair again tonight, are you?"

"No, I've promised my wife a kiss on the lips as soon as I get home."

"She's counting on you."

After the call, Chase rummaged around in the refrigerator for something to eat. Karla had gone out of her way with breakfast. Probably because it was so rare when they had the chance to eat together in the morning. She made blueberry muffins, scrambled eggs and ham, a short stack of pancakes, orange juice and coffee. It had looked incredible, but after only a bite or two Chase couldn't bring himself to eat any more. Why she hadn't given him a hard time about it, he'd never know.

He came across the ham-and-cheese sandwich from last night, gave it a try, and there it was again . . . the distaste. It wasn't as if he felt full or like he might throw up. Instead, it was a weird sense of disgust. The idea of trying to get something down . . .

Chase rewrapped the sandwich for a second time, and put it back in the refrigerator.

He'd eat when he was hungry; when food had some appeal again.

All the Lonely People / 36

4

Three o'clock rolled around and caught Chase by surprise. He'd sat down in the recliner for a quick nap, still trying to catch up on the sleep he'd lost last night. The next time he opened his eyes Oprah was on and evening clouds were moving across the sun outside. His grandmother once told him that when you lose sleep you can never get it back again. That seemed to be proving true. He felt exhausted, and now he was running late.

On his way to the bar, Chase stopped at the Rite Aid to pick up a sleep mask. He wasn't sure if it would help, it seemed to him that his trouble sleeping hadn't had much to do with the light bothering him, but since the sunglasses helped during the day, he figured it was worth a shot. The mask ran thirteen dollars. A bargain if it did the trick.

By the time he opened the front door to The Last Stop, it was a quarter to four.

There were empty mugs and half-empty bottles scattered throughout the place. Someone had left a jacket in one of the booths. Someone else had been in such a rush that he left a handful of change sitting untouched on a table. Chase had even forgotten to unplug the jukebox, which he normally did every night to cut down on his

David B. Silva / 37

electric bills.

People could hardly wait to get out of here last night. Why was that?

What the hell had that old man's box done to everyone?

Chase closed the door, flipped the switch to the neon lights in the window—Bud Light and Coors, as well as the OPEN sign—and hung his coat on the coat rack.

There was something else he noticed right away . . . the beer the old man had hardly touched. Last night, Chase had thought it odd, the way the man had nursed that drink, but maybe it hadn't been odd after all. It seemed likely, looking back on what had happened, that he had come here for something else entirely.

Behind the counter, Chase put on an apron and dumped the old man's beer. Over the next two hours he cleaned up the rest of the dishes, replaced the peanuts and pretzels, washed tables, paid some bills and made a few calls to suppliers. He hadn't thought much of the fact that no one had been waiting for him to open—sometimes you'd get a few early birds, but most of the regulars came in after five—but by the time he finished with all the busy work it was going on six and he was beginning to wonder where everyone was. It was Thursday night. ESPN was carrying a game between the Dolphins and the Bills. The walls should have been vibrating from the racket, like they did on Monday night games.

Chase poured himself a 7-Up, took it to a booth, and settled in to watch the game.

Maybe they were still feeling the effects from last night? That would explain it. Maybe they felt as exhausted as he felt. Or maybe it was just a fluky night when everyone was busy with other things. Those nights happened. Not often, but they did happen.

Jesus, who was he kidding?

There were no other *things*.

Something bad had happened.

All the Lonely People / 38

5

When Chase was seven, he fell off the jungle gym at school during recess. He could still remember his hands slipping from the bars. After that, everything had gone black until he opened his eyes and the school nurse was standing over him, surrounded by the faces of his classmates. He had been out for close to three minutes, which was why he ended up spending the night in the hospital. Just to be on the safe side, the doctor had said. Concussions could be a little tricky.

What had happened during those three minutes would forever be lost to him. He would never know what he did or what he said. That time had ceased to exist.

Just like the time between the end of the football game and now.

It was two-thirty in the morning.

Chase was sitting in the recliner in the living room. The lights were off. The AMC was running an old black-and-white Charlie Chan movie, with the sound turned down. The sweet smell of Karla's special spaghetti sauce was in the air, lingering hours after dinner, like it always did.

The catch was . . . Chase couldn't remember how he had gotten here.

David B. Silva / 39

Somehow, he'd managed to close the bar—at least he hoped he had—drive home, and plop down in front of the television. He'd done all this without any recollection of a single moment.

Now *that* was eerie.

Once . . . maybe he could chalk it up to just one of those things. Bad food or the cold weather, something like that. But this was *what*? The second or third time now? That was a red flag going up. It was a sign of a health problem. A medical problem. Or worse . . . a psychological condition.

He started to sit forward, but fell back.

Another headache.

This one was just above his eyebrows, extending to his hairline—which had begun to noticeably recede last year, something Danielle had playfully pointed out. The throbbing was so pronounced, Chase imagined if he looked in the mirror he would see his forehead expanding and contracting.

He rested his eyes a moment. When it became apparent the pain wasn't going to back off, he went upstairs after the ibuprofen. He'd already made the decision not to look at his reflection in the bathroom mirror. If his forehead was throbbing, he didn't want to see it. He pulled the bottle of 200 mg tablets from the cabinet under the sink and carried it back downstairs to the kitchen. Five didn't look like enough. He added three more and washed them down with half-a-glass of water.

Maybe that would help.

In the living room, Chase settled back into the recliner. The house was eerily quiet. He couldn't remember a time when he'd felt more alone. He turned the television down until he could barely hear the voices in the background. Then Chase closed his eyes . . . and drifted.

He hadn't even noticed he was still wearing sunglasses.

All the Lonely People / 40

PART IV:
TROUBLING ENCOUNTERS

1

Karla placed the palm of her hand over the sheet on her husband's side of the bed. The sheet was cold, the pillow fluffed, the blanket undisturbed. Two nights in a row now. What was going on?

She had gone to bed knowing better than to expect Chase to wake her with a kiss in the middle of the night, as he'd promised. That was something that just wasn't in him. Some men were romantics, some weren't. Chase saved his best for Valentine's Day, when he could always be counted on for a box of chocolates and a bouquet of flowers.

Still, a kiss in the middle of the night would have been nice.

Even nicer if Chase had slept in the bed next to her.

She got up, put on a pair of slippers and her robe, then went down the hall to her daughter's room. Danielle was sound asleep, half her body hanging over the edge of the bed, a position she seemed to gravitate to almost naturally when she was having difficulty breathing.

Karla shook her gently. "Time to get up, honey."

Danielle groaned.

"Come on, sleepy head." Karla yawned, and briefly thought how nice it would be if she could crawl into bed beside her daughter and sleep the morning away. "Don't make me dump a pail of cold water on you."

"You wouldn't." One eye opened, checking to see how serious things were.

"I would. And I'd enjoy it." Karla gave her daughter a swat on the behind, then went back down the hall, yawning, her eyes half-closed.

She took a longer-than-usual shower, wishing she could melt into the hot water. In the distance, behind the sound of the spray against the tile, she thought she could hear Danielle coughing. It wasn't unusual, of course. The sound of coughing came with the territory when your daughter had CF. But some coughs were worse than others, and Karla had been dealing with them long enough to know the difference.

She turned the water off and listened intently until Danielle began coughing again.

It didn't sound good.

Deep.

Phlegmy.

It sounded serious enough that they should probably get in to see the doctor.

Karla finished her shower. She toweled off, dried her hair, and dressed. She did a final check in the bathroom mirror. All the while, mentally she began to make adjustments to her schedule. If she picked Danielle up after school, they might be able to get in this afternoon. If the doctor had an opening. Or she could call in sick and take her into emergency.

Or Chase could take her.

Except he hadn't been himself the last day or two.

Her thoughts drifted effortlessly from Danielle to Chase, and she wondered if he was going through some sort of mid-life crisis. He was around that age. And lately they never seemed to have time for each other. Chase was busy with the bar. She was busy trying to make sure Danielle took care of herself. They were always running on parallel tracks that never seemed to cross.

All the Lonely People / 44

Karla dropped the damp towel in the hamper, and went down the hall. Danielle was still in bed, hanging over the edge, coughing. "Maybe we should keep you home today. That cough doesn't sound good."

"Mom, today's tryouts."

"There'll be other plays."

"No there won't. Not like this one. Melissa and Joanna were going to tryout with me. Besides, I'm always coughing."

Karla leaned against the door and studied her daughter.

"Please, Mom? Please, please, please, please."

With CF, there was such a fine line between a common cough and a lung infection. Karla hated taking the chance, but she also hated always playing the heavy. Every once in awhile, Danielle needed to be a little girl first; a little girl with CF second. There was nothing wrong with that, as long as they were careful.

"Please?" Danielle repeated.

"We'll see how you do with your therapy this morning."

"Thank you. Thank you. Thank you. You're the best Mom on the whole planet."

"Don't thank me yet, young lady. If you don't get up and get moving, I reserve the right to change my mind."

"On my way." Danielle jumped out of bed and raced past Karla down the hall to the bathroom

"And pack your flutter tube in case."

"I will."

Downstairs, Karla stopped to take a peak in the living room before she started breakfast. She expected to find Chase asleep in the recliner, where she had found him yesterday, and she did. The recliner was back, his feet were up. He was wearing a black mask over his eyes, something he'd never done before. If he'd been having trouble sleeping during the night, he seemed to be sleeping just fine now.

She nudged him. "Chase? You fell asleep in the living

David B. Silva / 45

room again."

He didn't move, except for the rise and fall of his chest with each new breath. At least there was that.

She nudged him again. "Chase?"

Still no reaction.

Karla watched him closely for a moment, trying to decide if she should let him sleep or if she should wake him just to make sure nothing was wrong. He'd always been a sound sleeper, but this seemed like more than a sound sleep. It was almost as if he were in some sort of comatose state.

"Chase? Come on, honey. Wake up for me."

Karla moved closer. His mouth was slack. There was spittle dribbling from one corner. His hair was clumped together where it had collected under the strap of the mask. He swallowed hard. Karla leaned in, pinched the corner of the mask between two fingers, and raised it.

His eyes were wide open.

It was a sight that both surprised and scared her.

A sharp gasp escaped her throat. She lost her grip on the mask. The black, velvety material snapped back into place with a sudden *pop!*

Chase let out a howl. His hands went to his face. He tore the mask away, startled, and sat up with a jolt. His eyes were huge and red and bloodshot. "What the hell did you do that for?"

Karla shook her head, one hand covering her mouth. "I'm so sorry. It's just . . . your eyes . . . you were sleeping with your eyes open. You scared the daylights out of me, Chase. I thought maybe you were . . ."

She was going to say *dead*, she thought maybe he was dead or something, but she caught herself.

"That hurt," Chase said. "That really . . ."

Then he appeared to fall instantly back to sleep again.

All the Lonely People / 46

2

A lack of air brought Chase awake.

He snorted and sat forward in the chair, wiped the spittle from his chin. The sleep mask lay in his lap, where he remembered dropping it after . . . Karla had woken him. Yes, he remembered that. Vaguely, but he remembered it.

Chase scratched absently at an itch on his forearm, then gradually acclimated to the familiar surroundings.

The television was on, its images bouncing light off the walls and closed curtains all around him. The sound was either off or turned so low Chase couldn't hear it. It was difficult to tell, because his ears were ringing with a deafening sound that reminded him of crickets in the night. Not just ringing, they were *screaming* at him.

He cleaned out one ear with his little finger, then tried popping his jaw. That seemed to help some. At least enough so he could think straight. Or as straight as he'd been able to think lately.

He had been talking to Karla, and he remembered how she had been upset about something. After that . . . well, after that things were still a little fuzzy.

Chase put aside the sleep mask, and picked up the sunglasses off the end table. He slipped them on. It was almost noon now. Sometimes the diamond-shaped Coors clock above the television ran a little slow, so it might be later than that, but probably not by much. That meant he'd been napping for what . . . nearly five hours? Christ, he couldn't sleep at night; and he couldn't seem to stay awake during the day.

And now you're sleeping with your eyes open, you psycho.

That's what Karla had been upset about. He remembered now. She said he'd been sleeping with his eyes open and it had nearly scared her half to death.

That sounded like the kind of thing that would have scared him half to death, too.

Sleeping with his eyes open. Weird. Nothing seemed normal anymore.

Nothing seemed *right*.

All the Lonely People / 48

3

Chase had a few errands to run before he met Karla for lunch at the Round Table Pizza next to the Raleigh's off Morningstar Road. He'd called her shortly after he woke and apologized for falling asleep.

"It was the oddest thing I've ever seen," she said over the phone. "Well, no, that had to be sleeping with your eyes open, but it was definitely a close second."

The thing that had struck her as so odd was that he had fallen asleep in the middle of a sentence. One second, he was talking, the next his head had lolled back against the chair and he was snoring.

"I wonder if that's where the phrase, bored to death, came from?" she said lightly.

Chase apologized again, reiterating that he was having a little trouble sleeping at night, but there was no reason to believe it wasn't temporary. Karla suggested he try an over-the-counter sleeping pill.

That was why his first stop had been at the Rite Aid. From there, Chase had gone by the post office and the bank. Now he was across the street from his last stop before lunch . . . Timber's Hardware.

He plugged a quarter in the parking meter, a brilliant idea by the City Council last year to raise extra funds to

David B. Silva / 49

upgrade the police department's fleet of aging vehicles, and dodged traffic crossing from one side of the street to the other. As Chase arrived at the front door, Ben Tucker came out of the hardware store empty handed. His eyes were downcast, and there were tufts of gray hair wildly sticking out from beneath the edges of an old painters cap.

"Ben!"

His friend looked up quickly, then glanced away. There were dark circles under his eyes, and Chase thought, *I bet I know what's going on with you, old friend. I bet your aren't sleeping a wink, are you?*

"You missed the game last night," Chase said. "Miami/Buffalo."

"Yeah, well, I was busy is all."

"I think everyone in town was busy."

"Yeah. Maybe so." Ben glanced up the street, one hand stuck in his mouth as he chewed nervously on his fingernails. They were already below the quick, raw and bleeding.

"It's happening to you, too, isn't it?" Chase asked.

Ben raised his head slightly, almost as if he were fighting with the last of his strength, but couldn't bring himself to make eye contact. "Happening? Nothing's happening."

"You haven't been having trouble sleeping?"

"I sleep."

"No nightmares?"

"Look, I gotta get going, all right?" Ben motioned up the street, where his Chevy pickup was parked at the curb. "Got lots to do, and time's running out."

"You don't look good," Chase said, and it occurred to him that he'd heard that somewhere else recently.

"I'm fine, really. Sorry to be rude, but there's only so many hours in a day." He nodded to himself, still chewing on those bloody fingernails, and started up the street in short, choppy steps that were entirely uncharacteristic of the man Chase had always known. It was like watching a

All the Lonely People / 50

shy, timid man rush to escape the eyes of the crowd after he'd dropped a platter at a social function. Ben Tucker had never been a timid man. He'd never been someone to turn away from a good conversation. Especially after his wife had died.

Chase shaded his eyes—even with sunglasses and the overcast it was bright out—and watched him climb into the pickup, looking thin and delicate. Like a shadow of the man Chase had known two nights ago. The Chevy pulled away from the curb, the left rear tire running over a discarded Orange Crush can.

When the truck was finally out of sight, Chase shook his head, turned around, and went into the hardware store.

Frank Weller was working behind the front counter. He was a tall, lanky kid in his early twenties. Chase knew his dad from the Oak Hill's Medical Center where the man worked as a lab technician. He'd drawn Danielle's blood on a number of occasions. He was her favorite because he could do it without it hurting.

"Hey, Chase."

"Frank." Chase leaned against the counter. "I've got a urinal that's leaking around the water connection. I've changed out the washer and the O Ring, but it's still leaking and I'm tired of fooling with it. Thought maybe you had something I could use to seal the joint."

"You just want it to stop leaking? You don't care how it looks?"

"Ugly's fine by me."

"You could try a sealant. It shouldn't look too bad." He came around the counter and took Chase back to the plumbing department.

"Saw Ben Tucker on my way in."

"You get a chance to talk to him?"

"A moment or two," Chase said. "He didn't have much to say."

"I don't think he's feeling well." They arrived in plumbing and Weller began to sort through the options.

"He looked like hell. Did you get a look at his hands? They're going to be stubs if he keeps chewing on them like that. I told him he should see a doctor."

"What did he say?"

"Something about not having any time."

"Said the same to me." Chase picked up a tube of plumbing compound and absently read the directions on the back. His interest had shifted away from the urinal problem; now he was curious why Ben had come into the store. "He buy anything? He wasn't carrying a bag."

Weller laughed. "You know what he wanted? Bricks and mortar mix."

"You're kidding? He say what for?"

"A backyard barbecue, he said. But that was all bullshit. He could build a barbecue in every backyard in the neighborhood with what he ordered."

At the front of the store, the bell over the door rang as someone entered. Weller looked up. He flipped a tube of Kitchen And Bath Silicone in the air, caught it and handed it to Chase. "Here. This should do the job."

"You guys don't carry brick and mortar, do you?"

"No, I ordered the stuff through Axner's. They're supposed to deliver it this afternoon." Weller gave him a pat on the back. "Excuse me, will you? I better check in case someone needs some help."

"Sure." Chase replaced the plumbing compound on the shelf and skimmed the back of the silicone tube. An odd uneasiness sat in the pit of his stomach. It sounded as if Ben were preparing for something big.

Then again, maybe Weller had it wrong.

Maybe the brick and mortar were for a barbecue.

All the Lonely People / 52

4

Karla appeared at the pizza parlor ten minutes early and was surprised to find Chase already there and waiting. She slid into the booth across from him. "I already ordered. Hope that's okay."

"No, that's fine. Glad you did. I only have half-an-hour. What did you get?"

"Half vegetarian, half pepperoni."

"Perfect." She slipped the purse off her shoulder, placed it next to her, and took a drink from her iced tea. Half-an-hour was going to be a little tight, but it seemed like she was always rushed these days. "Danny—"

"Danielle," Chase said.

"*Danielle*," Karla repeated. She wasn't sure how long it was going to take her to get used to the change. She'd always had a fondness for the abbreviated Danny. But Danielle was getting to that age when she seemed sensitive about everything, and having to go by a boy's name had been particularly touchy. "I think she might have an infection starting up. She coughed up an awful lot of junk this morning. I probably should have taken her to the doctor instead of letting her go to school."

"You worry over her too much."

"Someone has to." Karla took a napkin from the

David B. Silva / 53

dispenser, wiped the condensation off the bottom of her glass and used the moisture to wipe the table in front of her. She did this absently, routinely, much the same as she often did at home when they were talking.

"You smother her."

"That's what she keeps telling me."

"See?"

"See what? She's not even ten, Chase. She's a little girl. She doesn't have a clue what's good for her and what isn't."

"All I'm saying is you need to give her a little breathing room. That's all." Chase shifted uncomfortably in his seat, and pushed the sunglasses higher on his nose. "Let her have some fun. If she gets—"

"I let her have fun. That's why I let her go to school today. They're having tryouts for the play." Karla took another napkin, dried the table in front of her, then crumpled the damp napkin into the dry one and placed them both aside. "It's not like I keep her locked in the basement. She has friends. She does things."

When Chase didn't respond—sometimes when they got into these kinds of discussions, usually about Danielle, he went into his shut-down mode—Karla glanced up. His mouth was a thin, straight line, his breathing shallow, nearly undetectable. There was no expression on his face. It was an empty slate, all the emptier behind those irritating sunglasses.

"Are you listening?"

No response.

Karla reached across the table and touched his hand. He didn't move for a moment, as if his reaction time were on delay. Then his fingers curled slightly and he pulled his hand away.

"Chase?"

"Sorry," he said. He straightened and a quick, uneasy smile crossed the thin, straight line of his mouth. "My thoughts drifted. What were you saying?"

"No. You've been doing this a lot lately, this zoning

All the Lonely People / 54

out routine. You need to tell me what's going on," Karla said. "When I touched your hand, you didn't even react. It was like you were having a seizure or something."

"I don't know what's wrong," Chase said. The pizza arrived, along with some garlic twists which he had neglected to mention. "Things have been weird the last couple days. I haven't been feeling right."

"Did you pick something up to help you sleep like I suggested?"

"Yeah, but I don't think it's a lack of sleep. Not entirely." He dipped a twist into one of the dressing cups, took a bite, washed it down with Pepsi, and dropped the remainder onto his plate. With the sunglasses, it was almost impossible to read his face. "This guy came into the bar the other night. An older guy. In his sixties. Just passing through, he said, but I think there was more to it than that."

Karla moved a slice of pizza onto her plate and wiped her fingers on a napkin. Chase's last few words resonated—*there was more to it that that*—and she thought: *There was more to Danielle's cough, too.* A mother had a sense about these things. She had been troubled by that cough all morning. It kept ringing in her head, like a warning bell going off. Even now, as Chase was talking about some old man in the bar (there was never a shortage of bar stories), Karla wondered if she should go directly from Round Table to Danielle's school and pick up her daughter. That would mean Danielle would miss out on the tryouts. And if the doctor didn't find anything wrong, well, it would probably be weeks before her daughter forgave her.

It's not your job to be her friend, Karla told herself.

"It was like a bomb had gone off and everyone was in a state of shock," Chase was saying.

"Uh-huh." Karla took a small bite of her pizza and wiped her hands on the napkin again. If she didn't pick up Danielle and they missed the beginning of an infection . . . but then again there were only a couple hours before

David B. Silva / 55

school let out. Danielle could attend the tryouts, and by then they'd have a better idea if there was a problem. That might be better all around.

"And when I bumped into Ben Tucker . . ."

"You need a vacation. That's what you need," Karla said. It was settled in her mind now. She would wait until after school to pick up Danielle and make a decision then. "You work at that place seven days a week, 365 days a year."

"It's been a vacation lately," Chase said softly. "The bar's been like a ghost town."

5

It was like a ghost town again.

Chase sat on a stool behind the counter, nearly lost in the shadows created by the dim lights (*no sense wasting electricity when no one's here but me*). His eyes were closed. He could hear the buzzing sound of one of the neon lights out front. A throbbing pain pounded out a regular rhythm at the back of his head. He'd already downed more than 2,000 mg of ibuprofen without any relief. If the headache didn't kill him, the pills probably would.

It would be almost merciful if he could keep his eyes closed and just sort of fade away.

His thoughts drifted back to his lunch with Karla. It wasn't a clear memory, but he thought he'd told her about the incident at the bar and how he hadn't felt quite right ever since. He *thought* he'd told her, but he wasn't sure. If he had, he wasn't sure she'd heard him. Which was an interesting turn of events. Usually Karla did the talking, and he did the tuning out.

Not something he was particularly proud of, but true just the same.

Chase leaned back against the wall on two legs of the stool, and for a brief moment, before it began to pound again, he found relief from the headache.

What the hell's wrong with you?

What's happening?

The same thing that's happening to Ben Tucker, he thought suddenly.

Outside the hardware store this morning, Ben had seemed scattered and distracted. Chase hadn't known what to make of it at the time, but looking back now he realized that was the way he'd been feeling lately. It was like the confusion after a car accident, when you're stunned and you aren't thinking right. The adrenalin's pumping. You're stumbling around, trying to figure out what happened and if you're hurt. You're bruised and cut, and your entire body feels like it belongs to someone else. The last few days, Chase had been stumbling around, feeling like his entire life belonged to someone else. It was that confusion that had put the dark shadows under Ben Tucker's eyes, and it had done the same to Chase.

His eyes shot open. He took the weight off the back of the stool and sat forward.

He needed to call Ben Tucker. That's what he needed to do. This thing, whatever it was, they had it in common. Chase wasn't alone, they were both infected. And it probably wasn't just them. Maddie and Sam had been there, too. And Herb Canfield. And James Cleaver. They had all been there. They were all likely infected, all going through the nightmare.

Chase climbed off the stool. He was faintly aware of something building in the background, a sort of preparation for something that was coming. He'd experienced this before, during those wild and wacky puberty years. He hadn't understood it then, and he didn't understand it now, but something was changing inside him. It was taking place in miniscule shifts that were hardly noticeable, but it *was* taking place.

In the back office, where it always felt stuffy and confining, Chase pulled the worn chair up to the desk. He cleared a space for the Rolodex out of a pile of unpaid bills

All the Lonely People / 58

and notes scribbled on scraps of paper. Ben Tucker was the last card under the "T's." Chase popped it out of the file, sat back, and dialed the number.

The phone rang half-a-dozen times before Ben picked it up. "Quit bothering me! You hear? Just leave me alone!"

"Ben? It's Chase."

"There's nothing for you here!"

"It's Chase. From down at the bar. I bumped into you this—"

The line went dead.

Chase replaced the receiver and stared at the phone a moment, debating if he should give it another try. He wasn't sure there was any point. Ben Tucker hadn't sounded like a man who could be reasoned with. Still . . .

Chase redialed the number. He sat back and closed his eyes, wondering how long it would be before he started to sound like a raving lunatic, too. Was that where this was going? Down the river of no return?

The line was busy.

Apparently Ben had taken his phone off the hook.

PART V:
BRICK AND MORTAR

1

For the third or fourth morning in a row—they were starting to run together now—Chase opened his eyes to find himself stretched out on the recliner in the living room. He had a vague recollection of Danielle coughing and Karla harping on her about being late for school. But that was a scene that played often in this house. He couldn't be sure if it had happened on this particular morning or not.

The house was eerily quiet.

Chase dragged himself upstairs, feeling the pounding in his head start up. He splashed some water on his face, downed a few ibuprofen, and went back downstairs. He didn't bother with breakfast. The idea of eating continued to lack appeal. He grabbed his keys off the counter in the laundry room, and went out the door to the garage.

Chase settled in behind the wheel of the car, in the cool dark shadows, and realized he didn't know where he was going.

There was something he needed to do. He wasn't sure what it was, it escaped him at the moment, but it was important, he knew that.

He glanced in the rearview mirror, blinked, and . . .

Time shifted.

Another lapse, Chase thought. *Not a bad one, but a lapse just the same.*

It hadn't been long, only a few minutes.

He might not have noticed it, except for the bank of sunlight coming in through the little window in the door to the backyard. One moment it was a thin line catching the left corner of the hood of the car, the next it was five times the size and looked like a racing stripe down the middle. All in the blink of an eye.

Definitely a *lapse*.

Chase let out a long sigh, not unnerved as much as disheartened. He felt tired now, weary, felt like he wanted to close his eyes and drift for awhile.

If you close your eyes, you're going to sink to the bottom. Who knows how deep that could be? You might not come up again for hours.

Maybe days.

You might not come up ever again.

With that thought, he forced himself to move. Chase reached for the garage door opener first, pressed the gray button, and came further awake at the sound of the door rising. He started up the engine, rolled down the windows on both sides, and turned on the radio.

That was better. Much better.

A cool breeze came whispering through. His blood began to flow again.

And he remembered now, what he had needed to do today. He needed to go by and see Ben Tucker. If the call last night had told Chase anything, it had told him that Ben was worse off than he was. Far worse off. Chase needed to find out just how bad things were going to get.

All the Lonely People / 64

2

From the curb, nothing was particularly striking about the front of Ben Tucker's house. Not at first glance.

It was a ranch-style, with a two-car attached garage on one end, a small step-up porch with double-doors, and windows across the front that were hidden behind a mix of juniper and escallonia.

Chase had never been to the house before, which suddenly struck him as a sorry statement. He had attended Evelyn Tucker's funeral services, and had personally relayed his condolences to Ben, but he'd skipped the reception afterward so he wouldn't miss opening the bar at its regular time.

It was a nice house, though. Well kept on the outside.

The Chevy pickup was parked in the drive, so it was a fair bet Ben was home.

Chase knocked on the front door, and waited. When no one answered, he went around the side, next to the garage, where he found a gate. It took some doing to before he was able to flip the latch. Then he followed the yard past a line of garbage cans and an old wheel barrel leaning against the side of the house, around to the back.

Just beyond the corner, he nearly walked right past the first window, but something caught his eye. Chase stopped and tried to make sense of what he had noticed. The curtains didn't look right. For just a moment, he

David B. Silva / 65

thought it was because they were red and in sharp contrast to the light green color of the house. Then he realized they weren't curtains at all. The windows had been bricked over from the inside.

Further along, the first sliding-glass door, which opened onto the back porch, was also bricked over.

And the double-windows after that.

"Jesus," Chase muttered. "What the hell's he doing?"

At the far end of the porch, the second sliding-glass door had several rows of bricks before it would be sealed, too. Chase watched a hand reach up from the murk on the other side, add a brick to the top row, and tap it into place with the end of a trowel.

"Ben? It's Chase. Getting a little claustrophobic in there?"

"Go away, Chase." Muffled by the glass door and the brick wall, he sounded as if he were standing deep in the heart of a cave. "There's nothing you can do."

"I know what you're going through."

"No, you don't. No one knows."

"The headaches. Losing time. Feeling like something's missing, like you aren't all quite there."

Ben Tucker laughed and the sound sent a chill through Chase. "That it? That everything that's happened to you up to now? Hate to tell you, buddy old pal, but that's nothing. That's the flat tire before the whole damn truck takes a header off the cliff. It's the bottom of the drop that really gets you."

"You don't want to do this, Ben. What's the point?"

Another brick went onto the top row. As Ben tapped it into place with the handle of the trowel, Chase caught a quick glimpse of the top of Ben's head. Yesterday, he had been wearing that old painter's cap and wild tuffs of gray hair had been sticking out from underneath. Now, Chase understood why. Ben had been literally pulling his hair out. There were bald patches on both sides and across the top, mixed with wild gray tuffs that had somehow managed to survive up to now.

All the Lonely People / 66

"Come on, don't do this."

The handle of the trowel came to rest against one end of the last brick, Ben's gloved hand wrapped around its shank, neither moving.

It's a lapse, Chase thought. *Ben's fallen into a lapse.*

For a moment, all Chase could think to do was wait and hope it didn't last long. But he didn't like the feel of standing around waiting and in a short time an idea came to him.

"Ben? You hear me? You all right?"

When his friend didn't respond, Chase returned to the car for his cell phone. He dialed 911 and told the operator that some guy was barricading himself inside his house and that he might be suicidal. That wasn't true, of course—at least Chase didn't believe it was true, not yet anyway—but it seemed close enough to the truth that he didn't mind saying it. He gave her the address, then hung up and went back around the side yard to the back porch.

The *lapse* had been a short one.

Ben added another brick to the wall as Chase watched.

"What are you afraid's going to happen?"

"If you'd seen what I've seen, you'd be afraid too," Ben said. He said this without skipping a beat, with the trowel disappearing behind the wall and another brick arriving on top.

"What about food and water?"

"Already stocked up."

"How long are you planning to hole up in there?"

"Long as it takes."

As long as what takes? Chase wondered. "This is nuts, Ben."

Another brick went onto the wall.

Chase pulled up a patio chair and sat down. It was an unusually warm day for this time of year, easily above seventy. The sky was clear. The sun was at its peak, riding a little lower in the southern sky than it did in the middle of summer. Even with sunglasses, the glare was painful.

David B. Silva / 67

"I called the cops."
"Won't do no good."
"We'll see."

All the Lonely People / 68

3

While Chase waited for the police to arrive, he took a walk around the perimeter of the house. Ben had bricked over every last window. Most likely every door, too, though there was no way to know for sure. The front door was locked. The side door to the garage was open, but the door between the garage and the house was also locked. A pile of palettes and empty sacks of mortar mix sat in the middle of the garage floor. Chase kicked at the nearest sack and sent it sliding across the concrete slab just as the bell rang at the front door.

Two patrol cars were parked at the curb, one slanted sideways in back of his car, as Chase came around the yard. There were two officers on the stoop, another hanging back ten or twelve feet, his thumbs tucked into his belt as if he were assuming a pose for a local newspaper photographer.

"You the one who called in the suicide?"

"Not a suicide yet. I'm just worried that's how it might play out." Chase stuck out his hand and the nearest officer, a broad-shouldered and slightly overweight man with a humorless face, offered his own. "Name's Chase. The man inside is Ben Tucker."

"So what's the problem?"

"He's barricading himself inside the house." Chase pushed aside an escallonia bush that was blocking a window. "See? All the windows are like this. He's sealed them all."

"This his place?"

"Yeah."

"Anyone else inside?"

"No. He lives alone."

"He make any threats? Talk about killing himself?"

"Well, no. Not exactly." Chase shifted uneasily in place, doing his best to keep his voice even and his eyes from drifting. "Just talk to him. That's all I'm asking. Talk to him and see what you think. He's right around back, bricking up the last sliding-glass door."

Chase led them around the house to the back porch.

Ben had been a busy man. He'd finished another row of bricks. The space between the wall and the top of the glass door was a narrow slit now, too small to accommodate a small child much less a grown man.

The cop with the humorless face (his name was Ecker according to the brass name plate above his shirt pocket) spoke up as Ben added another brick to the wall. "Mr. Tucker? I'm with the Mercury Police Department. You want to tell me what you're doing?"

"Home repairs," Ben said.

"Bricking up your windows?"

"Is there something I can help you with, officer?"

"Your friend here's expressed concern about you."

"He's not my friend."

Chase ran a hand through his hair, and absently wondered how long it would be before he started pulling his own hair out like Ben. "Jesus, Ben, quit screwing around. You know you can't stay in there."

"He's the reason I'm in here, officer." Another brick went onto the top row. It was painstakingly tapped into place. "He threatened me."

Ecker turned to Chase. "That true?"

"Of course not."

"I'm behind on my bar tab," Ben said without missing a beat. There was no life in his voice. It was flat and

All the Lonely People / 70

unemotional. It was also very convincing. "Said he wanted to make an example of me."

"You own a bar?" Ecker asked.

"Yeah. The Last Stop. Out off—"

"I know the place."

"Check his eyes," Ben said. "I think he's on something."

"That's not funny!" Chase shouted.

Ecker motioned at the sunglasses. "You mind taking 'em off?"

"My eyes . . . they're a little sensitive to the sunlight," Chase said. "Christ, Ben, tell 'em you're only bullshitting 'em."

"Please remove the sunglasses, sir."

This was insane. All he'd wanted was to make sure Ben didn't do anything crazy. Now this. Shading his eyes, Chase slid the sunglasses down his nose and away from his face. Instantly, a deep dull ache burrowed into his pupils. He turned away, squinting, his eyes watering.

"I need to see your pupils," Ecker said.

"Give me a second." Chase blinked a few times. The pain didn't get any worse, but it didn't get any better, either. He'd been hit in the eye with a football once, in junior high, while trying to block a pass, and the pain had been just like this. Dull and deep and lingering. It had stayed with him through the night and well into the next day, and like now the only time he'd felt relief was when his eyes were closed. Chase struggled to keep them open long enough for the cop to have a look.

"They're fully dilated," Ecker said.

"Told you," Ben said.

"You taking anything? Any medications?"

"No, of course not," Chase said, slipping the sunglasses on again. "Just a ton of ibuprofen."

"Uh-huh. Mind if we check your pockets?"

Chase minded, he minded plenty, but he didn't protest. The hole he'd dug himself was deep enough, he didn't want to dig it any deeper. He emptied his pockets, pulling out his wallet, the keys to the car, some change, then turned the pockets inside out. Unsatisfied, Ecker asked if it would be okay to take a look inside his car. Chase agreed to that search, too, suddenly anxious just to get this mess over with and behind him.

Once the cops were satisfied he wasn't using or dealing, they dawdled around for a time before Ecker finally apologized for the inconvenience. He thanked Chase for his cooperation, and that seemed to be the end of it. The other two officers climbed into their patrol car and drove off. Ecker finished writing some notes, and started toward his car as well.

"What about my friend?" Chase asked.

"It's his house. He's not doing anything illegal." Ecker paused at the door of the cruiser. "If I were you, I'd leave him alone. If he wanted, he'd be well within his rights to file a complaint against you for trespassing or harassment. You'd be wise to let it go. Just get in your car and be on your way."

Eventually, that was exactly what Chase did, but first he went back around the house to try one last time to talk to Ben. There were only a few brick-sized spaces left to fill now. Then the glass door would be completely sealed. Even the top of Ben's head was no longer visible behind the brick wall.

"Last chance, Ben."

"They didn't haul you off?"

"No thanks to you," Chase said.

"You would have been safer in jail."

"Safer from what?"

"You'll find out soon enough, I imagine." The trowel came up out of the shadows and filled the space between two bricks with mortar. "For your sake, I hope I'm wrong."

Then the final brick slid into place.

All the Lonely People / 72

4

The image of the last brick sliding into place stayed with Chase the rest of the day. It was with him when he climbed into the car outside Ben Tucker's house and momentarily closed his eyes before driving off. It was with him after he'd opened the bar and settled into another lonely night. And it was with him now, as he suddenly became aware that he was sitting at the kitchen table, across from Karla.

She was *not* wearing a happy face.

Chase smiled just the same, doing his best to cover the fact that he had no idea where he'd been or what he'd been doing since his recollection of being at the bar.

Through the kitchen window, he could see it was dark out. Karla was dressed as if she were ready for bed, so she must have waited up for him. Or he might have come home early, since it had continued to be nearly tomb-like at The Last Stop. He didn't think he'd be going back there again. It felt almost as if the bar were losing its memory, too. As if it no longer had a history.

"I know you love the bar," Karla said evenly. She was dressed in a pink robe over her pajamas. Her hair was bobby-pinned on both sides—*it keeps it from getting tangled at night*, she'd told him early in their marriage—and she'd already cleansed her face of what little makeup she wore. "And I'm glad you're passionate about it."

"But?"

"But . . . if you aren't going to take an interest in Danielle, the very least you could do is offer me some support. Every time she runs to you about something, you give in to her. She won't even listen to me anymore."

Chase nodded. He wasn't sure what had happened, but apparently it was the same old story. Danielle had wanted to do something and her mother had pulled out the CF card and said no. So Danielle had come running to him. She may only be nine, but she was already a master at pitting them against each other. It didn't take much. It seemed to Chase (it had *always* seemed to Chase) that their daughter needed to hear what she *could* do, instead of always being told what she *couldn't*. But tell that to Karla.

"What are you so afraid of?" Chase asked.

Karla's back straightened. "Jesus, Chase, what do you think I'm afraid of?"

"You can't be with her every minute of everyday. You can't protect her from the world."

"I can try. That's more than you do."

That much was true; and they both knew it was true. Even so, for a moment Chase was tempted to try to defend himself, however thin the ice he was standing on. "No. Don't you see? You can't do it for her. You need to let her grow her own strength so she can do it for herself."

"And when she ends up in the hospital because she hasn't been taking care of herself, what then? Am I supposed to pretend that everything's okay, that it's no big deal?" Karla got up from the table, dumped what coffee remained in her cup down the sink, and ran the water. "Besides, this really isn't about me. It's about you."

It's always about me, Chase thought.

Karla returned to the table, her lips tight, her eyes narrow. "I don't know what's going on with you, but it's like you're never really here anymore. You come and go as if you were renting a room. Sometimes I wonder . . ."

All the Lonely People / 74

"There isn't," Chase said. She looked up at him, uncertain. For a moment he felt as focused and as connected as he had felt in a long, long time. "There's no one else."

Relief crossed her face. "Because if there is . . ."

"There isn't."

"Then what is it, Chase? What's going on?"

"I'm not sure."

Just don't be surprised if sometime soon I start to brick up the doors and windows.

Chase stared out the kitchen window at the night, which seemed oppressively dark. If he really understood what was going on, Karla would be the person he would tell. She would be the one person in his life who would at least hear him out, even if she thought he was spouting a bunch of nonsense. But if he tried to explain what little he knew, what little he *understood*, it would only make things worse.

"You haven't . . ."

"What?" Chase asked. "Haven't what?"

Karla let out a slow, careful breath. "You haven't started drinking again, have you, Chase?"

Oh, that's great. Just great. He'd never been a serious drinker. Never. A few beers now and then. That was all. Except for that one time, just after Danielle had been diagnosed, when he'd felt the pressure building, and yeah, sure, he'd hit the bottle a little harder than he should have. But Karla had called him on it almost immediately, threatening to leave him if he didn't stop, and that had been the end of it. He couldn't even remember the last time he'd had a drink.

"No," Chase said. "I'm not drinking."

But the idea sure sounded nice.

PART VI:
ISOLATION

1

Maddie Ashburn pulled out the top drawer of her dresser, and let it drop to the floor under its own weight. One of the side panels snapped in two. A six inch splinter went flying off in the direction of the bedroom door. Maddie fell to her knees. She rummaged through the bras and panties, tossing them out as she dug deeper into the drawer.

It had to be here somewhere.

If only she could remember where she'd stored it.

When the drawer was empty, she pulled out the next drawer, then fell to her knees and frantically began to dig through the once-organized piles of socks and pantyhose. She had an idea that if she didn't find the photo album, and find it soon, all those memories captured on film would be lost forever. She needed them to remind her.

There was no photo album in the sock drawer.

No album in the blouse drawer, either.

Nor the pants drawer.

Shit, what had she done with it?

One sliding closet door lay propped against the wall, the other dangled dangerously on a single roller still clinging to the track. A pile of sweaters and dresses, coats and slacks covered most of the bed. A single plastic hanger, slightly misshapen from the weight of her belts, still hung in the closet. Indentations in the carpet at the bottom of the closet outlined where her shoes had once been stored. They were scattered haphazardly around the bedroom now, wherever they had landed as she'd tossed them aside.

Maddie took a quick inventory of the room, the piles of clothes, the empty shopping bags where she had found some old tax records and a mess of receipts she'd forgotten all about when she had done her taxes last year.

Under the bed.

She hadn't checked under the bed.

She couldn't remember the last time she'd cleaned under there, (hell, she couldn't remember much of anything lately), but it had been quite some time. There was a pair of slippers she thought she'd lost, and a hardcover edition of *Harry Potter and The Chamber of Secrets*. She'd never been able to finish the book, though she'd convinced herself it was probably because she needed to start the series at the beginning. For a moment, as she pulled it out from the dark recess, she felt a wave of relief wash over her. She was certain she'd found the photo album. When she realized it wasn't what she thought, she blew the dust off the cover, tossed the book aside, and climbed back to her feet.

This is just like you, losing something of value.

The voice didn't belong to her. It belonged to her father. He'd been dead for nearly fifteen years, after suffering through a series of strokes and an eventual heart attack, but he still talked to her whenever she felt under stress.

Maddie left the master bedroom and went down the narrow hall of the single-wide mobile home to the guest room. She had bought the place with the money from her divorce settlement eight, nearly nine years ago. There had been no children from the marriage (Maddie had had a hysterectomy in her early twenties due to some "female problems" as her mother euphemistically referred to them), which had been one of the reasons the marriage had eventually dissolved. It hadn't been the *only* reason,

All the Lonely People / 80

but it had been the *main* reason.

Now, she couldn't even remember his name.

Or what he looked like.

Or the last time she had seen him.

She slammed the sliding closet door against the stop. The closet had become a catchall since she'd first moved into the mobile home. She scooped up the rack of mostly summer clothes and dumped them on the bed. Two of her father's dress suits hung on the far side, next to what had been her mother's favorite dress before she had died. Maddie left them in the closet, and instead went down to her knees to sort through the mess on the floor. Piled in the corner were some old purses, old shoes she'd never had the heart to toss out, and four or five wig stands she'd picked up from the Good Will the year before last and had never used. These came flying out of the closet piece by piece as she dug through them.

Maddeningly, there was no photo album underneath.

Next, one by one, she pulled the sealed boxes off the top shelf and dumped them on the floor.

Maddie collapsed to the floor beside them and ripped open the top of the nearest box.

The photo album had to be here somewhere. It *had* to be.

The first box was filled with a collection of rag dolls. The second box contained a set of silverware she had last used for Thanksgiving dinner a number of years ago (she couldn't remember how many years ago, just that it had been a long time). Another box was stuffed with linens. Another with off-color pearl necklaces, oversized broaches, and outlandish earrings she hadn't worn since . . . since when? Her early twenties? Her teens?

Maddie kicked at the box and collapsed back against the floor. She stared at the ceiling, feeling it growing inside her . . . that sense of being lost, of being disconnected from the world around her. With every breath, it seemed as if a little more of her disappeared.

The album wasn't in the closet.

David B. Silva / 81

Nor in the dresser, or under the bed.

With tears running down her face—because she was almost certain now she wasn't going to find it, no matter where she looked—Maddie made her way down the hall to the bathroom and began to ransack the linen closet.

It wasn't there, either.

Maybe there had never been a photo album. That was possible, wasn't it?

Maybe it was something her mind had made up, the way it sometimes made up a false picture of where she'd left the car keys or how many drinks she'd had down at The Last Stop.

No, no, no. There was a photo album. There *had* to be a photo album.

Maddie, who had been sitting on the bathroom floor, surrounded by linens, climbed back to her feet and went down the hall to the living room.

It was a small space, with a floral-patterned sofa pushed up against the wall at one end, and a short counter separating the room from the kitchen at the other. She plopped down on the sofa and stared at the black-and-white television set mounted on the imitation oak hutch. She didn't have much of a collection of movies on VHS tape, but those few that she'd bought over the yeas, she kept in the hutch.

And suddenly the picture in her mind seemed clear again.

She had also kept the photo album in there, hadn't she?

Yes, she had.

Maddie fell to her knees in front of the hutch, the shag carpet lumpy beneath her. She paused, almost too afraid of the disappointment to look, then slowly opened the doors.

And there it was.

Finally.

The photo album.

Almost exactly where she now remembered leaving it,

All the Lonely People / **82**

which was nearly as gratifying as actually finding it.

She closed her eyes and held the album against her breasts.

Thank you!

Then she opened the cover and studied the first picture. She was three, dressed in a little white jumpsuit and a bonnet, sitting on the stoop outside the back door of the house where she had grown up. For a moment, Maddie Ashburn could almost feel the sun against her face, smell the freshly-mowed lawn, hear the breeze toying with the leaves of the old oak in the backyard. For a moment, she felt whole again.

2

Karla leaned over the drinking fountain, her foot on the pedal, one hand holding the hair away from her face, even though she honestly wasn't thirsty. The cool water passed untasted and nearly unfelt over her lips before she wiped the back of her hand across her mouth and straightened up.

Danielle was down the hall in Room 346.

Karla tried not to think about it, but couldn't help herself.

Three days had passed since Danielle's cough had first sounded suspect. For a time, Karla had begun to think Chase had been right . . . she worried too much. But then last night, the coughing had brought up thick globs of dark, greenish mucus, almost always an early sign of a lung infection. It hadn't been quite as bad this morning, but it had been bad enough that she should have done something about it. Instead, she had let Danielle talk her into waiting until after school.

Never again.

Karla glanced up the hospital corridor at the nurse's station, which was painted in the same broad yellow-and-brown stripes that ran horizontally down the center of the walls. A woman in a white nurse's uniform leaned against the counter, reading a chart, her feet crossed casually at the ankles. Another nurse, this one sitting behind the

All the Lonely People / 84

counter, was busy on the phone. An old man, wearing a dark blue robe over his hospital gown, shuffled slowly down the hall, one hand tugging on an IV pole on wheels.

God, how she hated hospitals.

It was sometime after seven, she guessed. Maybe as late as eight, she couldn't be certain. Time seemed to set its own schedule when her thoughts were preoccupied. The entire afternoon had gone by in a blur, and already seemed to be fading in the distance. Except for what the doctor had told her. That was still crystal clear in Karla's mind.

"If it was anyone else in her age group, without her medical history," he'd said, "then I'd probably let you take her home, as long as we took some basic precautions. But I don't think that's in her best interest at this point."

He hadn't been willing to predict how long Danielle would be in the hospital. Instead, he pointed out that both her heart rate and her temperature were running high, and those would have to show signs of improvement before they could even begin to entertain thoughts of releasing her.

When Karla had pressed him for his best guess, the doctor had grudgingly told her, "Could be three, five, maybe eight days, depending."

Now that she'd put it off as long as she could, Karla started back up the hall toward Danielle's room. She already dreaded the thought of seeing that unhappy, little-girl face. If she could, she'd wave a magic wand and instantly Danielle's life would be filled with joy, free from the CF that always seemed to taint things. But she had stopped believing in magic wands a long time ago. You just had to take one day at a time and hope for the best.

"Karla! Hold up!"

It was Chase.

She turned around at the sound of his voice, and nearly didn't recognize him. He was still wearing those same irritating sunglasses, which she'd given serious thought to shoving down the garbage disposal, and the

David B. Silva / 85

same clothes he'd worn the last three or four days straight. A pair of loose-fitting Levis, a plaid long-sleeved shirt, and a Giants jacket. But he hadn't shaved recently, and there was a drawn, hollow defeat in his face.

"Got your message," Chase said as he caught up with her. "How is she?"

"Where have you been? I called the house, the bar . . ."

"Running errands."

"Who's watching the bar?"

"Right now? No one. I closed up."

They walked a few steps together, side by side, as if they were taking a stroll through the park, then Karla stopped abruptly. She turned to him, trying to read through that hollow defeat. It wasn't like Chase to close the bar. Not for anything. Not for anyone. "Really? You closed up?"

"Is she okay?"

"Yeah," Karla said evenly. "She'll be all right. It's a lung infection. Nothing serious. Par for the course, the doctor said."

"Then why are they keeping her?"

"Because your daughter has cystic fibrosis," she said. She'd almost laughed, until she realized he hadn't been joking. "They want to play it safe and make sure it doesn't turn into anything more serious."

Chase nodded.

She studied her reflection in the dark lenses of his sunglasses, curious about what was going on behind them. "You look godawful."

They began to walk again, edging past the nursing station.

"I'm all right."

"Still aren't sleeping, are you?"

"Not much."

"Where were you last night? Thought I'd find you downstairs in the recliner this morning. You sleep at the bar?"

All the Lonely People / 86

"How long they going to keep her?"

"A few days," Karla said.

"She's all right, though. Right?"

"They've got her on antibiotics."

"Good." He nodded slightly, and adjusted the sunglasses on his face. "That's good."

"You aren't staying, are you?"

"Are you?"

"Of course, I am. She's my daughter." Karla had called from the doctor's office and arranged to take the next few days off. One of the nurses was going to move a cot into the room tonight so Danielle wouldn't have to sleep alone in a strange place. "She needs me."

One corner of Chase's mouth curled into a soft smile, then disappeared back into the straight thin lines of his face. For a brief moment, it was almost as if he were human. "You were right. She does need someone to keep an eye on her."

Karla nodded. "Thank you."

They arrived at the room, a double with a sliding curtain between the adjoining areas. The bed closest to the door was unoccupied, though it wasn't likely to remain that way for long. Last week, the Mercury Record had run a story about the county's hospital bed shortage. As recent as last December there had been several occasions when Mercury Medical had been forced to send patients downstate to Sacramento. A new wing was already under construction, but it wasn't scheduled for completion until late next year.

Chase rounded the curtain with caution, as if he were afraid what he might find.

Karla stepped in behind him.

Danielle's face lit up instantly with a broad, gleeful smile. "Daddy!" She stuck out her arms to greet him. Chase moved around the bed and melted into the hug. He held on as if he were afraid to let go, as if it were for dear life, then reluctantly his arms fell away and he stepped back.

David B. Silva / 87

"How are you doing, pumpkin?"

"Okay."

"You eat dinner already?"

Her nose wrinkled. "They had string beans."

Chase nodded uncomfortably, and glanced out the window at the glitter of the town's lights in the night. He had worn an oddly sad smile as he had hugged his daughter, but the smile was gone now, replaced once again by that distant, hollow mask.

"Clear skies out tonight," Karla said.

"This nightgown itches," Danielle said. She'd hated changing out of her clothes into the hospital gown. The flaps in the back wouldn't close, which prompted a quick sprint from the bathroom to the bed. Buried under the sheets for a short time, when she finally popped her head out again, her face had been bright red with embarrassment.

"I think it's cotton," Karla said. She went around the bed to take a look at the tag, which didn't seem to exist. "It doesn't say, but it *feels* like cotton."

Danielle tapped her on the arm and pointed at Chase.

Karla turned.

He looked like a snapshot in time, like a mannequin. Stiff. Ashen. His face impassive. His arms posed. This was what had happened the other night when he'd fallen asleep in the middle of a sentence. There was a medical term for it, she'd read about it somewhere, but Karla couldn't remember the word.

She put her hand on his arm. "Chase?"

"I think he's sleeping," Danielle said.

"You might be right."

"Is that really possible? Sleeping while you're standing up like that? I mean, wouldn't you lose your balance and fall over or something?"

"Maybe we should make sure he doesn't hurt himself," Karla said. She helped him to a chair in the corner and encouraged him to sit. It wasn't easy. His muscles were tense, his spine rigid. Even though she had

***All the Lonely People* / 88**

a fairly good idea what she would find, she removed the sunglasses from his face. Underneath, Chase's eyes were wide open. The pupils were fixed and dilated, almost lifeless. He looked like a cartoon character under some sort of hypnotic trance.

She shook his arm again. "Chase? Come on, honey, you're scaring us."

"Is he all right?" Danielle asked.

"I'm sure he's fine."

"Maybe we should call a nurse or somebody?"

Out in the hall, two people passed the open door in loud conversation. The distraction drew Karla's attention. She looked up, thinking Danielle had been right, and hoping to discover a nurse coming to check on her daughter. When that didn't turn out to be the case, she turned her attention back to Chase.

Suddenly, he was awake again, scratching at his forearm. "I hate this damn itching. It feels like it's eating me from the inside out. It's worse than poison oak."

"Are you all right, Daddy?"

"I'm fine, pumpkin. Just a little itchy is all."

Danielle giggled.

Karla kneeled next to the chair, one hand on her husband's arm. These little bouts were getting serious. He wasn't slipping into quick little catnaps to catch up with lost sleep; he was drifting into deeper territory. And it was happening more and more often. "You sure you're all right? You blanked out, Chase. Like you did the other night."

"I'm fine. Really." He smiled unevenly, less a smile than a grimace.

"Your arm bothering you?"

The moment she mentioned it, Chase stopped scratching. "It's just an itch. I can itch, can't I?"

"We can have a nurse take a look at it."

"It's not that bad."

Karla leaned into him and lowered her voice. "I don't know what's going on with these blackouts of yours . . ."

"They aren't blackouts."

"But you need to see a doctor. You shouldn't be nodding off in the middle of sentences, Chase. That's a sign that something's not right."

"There's nothing wrong."

"I'm not going to argue about it with you. We both know something's not right. Go see a doctor. If you don't want to do it for yourself, do it for your daughter." She gave him a pat on the arm, a peck on the cheek. "You mind making a trip home and bringing back a few games and books?"

"And Alfie!" Danielle screamed. "Don't forget Alfie!"

"Her stuffed lion," Karla said.

"No, not at all. I don't mind at all."

3

The engine was running.

The headlights were on low beam, striking the front of The Last Stop about waist high, where the used-brick facade stopped and the wood siding began.

The radio was tuned to KLIV 1400 AM, an oldies station. The tail end of *Good Vibrations* by the Beach Boys was winding down, with that weird sound you always heard in '50s horror flicks. Made with a theremin. Probably the only hit song that ever used one.

Chase gulped for a breath. It felt as if he'd just come up from the depths of the ocean. A burning sensation filled his lungs. His heart kicked at the inside of his chest until it almost hurt. His face was drenched in a cold sweat.

He took in another breath, shallower this time, and unwrapped his hands from the steering wheel.

How long had he been sitting here?

Hunkered down in thick night shadows, the bar looked like a dying beast, mired in muck with little hope of escape. Weeds were beginning to break through the cracks in the concrete porch. Paint was beginning to peel around the door. Around back, there was an old dumpster and the pavement was pocked with holes and debris that had been collecting for years. The light was bad there, and he'd convinced himself no one ever saw

David B. Silva / 91

that part of the building so it didn't matter. But now Chase knew the truth: the front of the bar looked nearly as bad.

Chase turned the engine off.

The radio fell silent.

He knew this much: he'd made the trip home to pick up some of Danielle's things, just like he'd promised Karla, and he'd made the trip back to the hospital to drop them off. He had done all that without incident. In fact, he could remember giving Danielle a hug and drawing the curtains across the window in her hospital room. And he remembered a middle-aged man with dark hair and wire-rimmed glasses, who at a glance looked healthy enough to run a marathon, being wheeled in on a gurney as he had been leaving.

But that was all Chase remembered of the evening.

Until now.

Chase jiggled the ignition switch until the dashboard lights came up. Simultaneously, *Walk Like A Man* by The Four Seasons came up on the radio. He checked the time. It was shortly after midnight. What did that mean? He'd lost some three-odd hours? How did you lose three hours?

The same way you lose five minutes.

One second at a time.

He had no idea how he'd ended up here, but he knew this much: there was no way he was going to open The Last Stop tonight. Not tomorrow night, either. Not unless things suddenly improved. Sooner or later, he was going to have to sit down with Karla and tell her the bar had gone belly up, and there had been nothing he could do about it. One day it had been packed with regular customers, the next it had been . . .

A ghost town.

Simple as that.

The idea of having to tell her such a thing did not have much appeal, a little like the idea of having to eat. At the same time, he imagined it might never come to that. Long before then, he'd probably end up bricking himself inside the bar and threatening to shoot anyone who bothered him.

That . . . or he'd be dead.

Chase turned the engine over, and shifted into reverse. He glanced over his shoulder at the black veil of night, and slowly backed out of the vacant lot. The road was deserted, not surprising for this time of night. To his right, he could see a stoplight in the distance, at the corner of Vanguard. The light was yellow, turning red. To his left, the white dotted line down the middle of the road gradually faded into the darkness until it disappeared altogether.

He had no destination in mind, just the idea that he needed to keep moving.

Chase turned left and accelerated.

4

Herb Canfield didn't hear the knock at the door.

Jerry Springer was on in the living room. In the spare bedroom, which Canfield used almost exclusively as an office, the small black-and-white Panasonic wasn't hooked up to the satellite dish and the reception was more snow than picture, but it was on, too, and the ghostly images of *Rome Is Burning* could be seen fading in and out like undulating heat waves. A rerun of *The X-Files* played on the 19-inch Zenith in the master bedroom.

The volume on each of the sets was turned up as high as it would go.

Another knock at the door went unheard.

Canfield took a long swig from his Red Dog, and dangled the bottle over the arm of the living room couch. His eyelids hung at half-mast. Behind them, a dull ache—the sort of pain that lingered long after you'd had a tooth pulled—had been gradually growing in strength throughout the day. It felt as if it might drive him over the edge if it went on much longer.

On *Springer*, some white trash, trailer park bimbo flashed her ass at the audience.

The play of shadow and light in the living room shifted as the picture changed.

A roar of laughter broke out.

Canfield took another drink, dimly aware of a sound

All the Lonely People / 94

that didn't appear to be coming from any of the sets. His head lolled back against the couch, the front door caught upside-down in his vision.

The knock came again, louder this time. It wasn't the sound so much that registered in Canfield's brain as it was the sight of the front door bulging inward with each new *thump*! He sat up, suddenly alert, his muscles tense, the dull ache behind his eyes momentarily shut out.

Someone was at the door.

He set the Red Dog on the floor, leaning against the side of the couch. Then he climbed to his feet and waited, hoping he'd been mistaken. When the knock came again, no doubt about it this time, he went to the door and peered through the eyehole. There were two policemen standing outside on the porch.

"What do you want?"

"Sir, we need to speak with you. We've received a complaint from one of your neighbors."

"Complaint about what?"

"The noise."

"I'll turn it down. I promise."

"We'll have to ask you to open the door, sir."

"I told you, I'll turn it down."

"Open the door *now*, sir."

The pain behind his eyes returned, stronger now, feeling as if someone were hammering against the inside of his skull. Canfield leaned against the door with his head and sighed. It wasn't looking like he had much of a choice. Slowly, he opened a crack in the door.

The nearest police officer flashed a light in his face. "What's your name?"

Canfield winced. "Herb. Herb Canfield."

"You throwing a party in there, Herb?"

"No, it's just me."

"Mind if we come in and have a look around?"

"Look, I'm sorry about the neighbors," Canfield said. "I'll turn it down. Honest."

"I think we need to have a look around first." With a

David B. Silva / 95

flashlight in hand, the officer—a black man, thin, with a clean-shaven face and eyes that looked as if they rarely missed anything—moved across the threshold.

Canfield stepped back from the door.

"Why are all the lights off?" the officer asked. His voice was controlled but forceful and barely audible above the television. He swept the beam of his flashlight down Canfield's body in one smooth motion, then up again and settled on Canfield's face.

"I've got a headache. It helps if I keep the lights low."

"Maybe if you turned the racket down?"

The second officer—a tall, lanky man who looked like a strong wind might pick him up and carry him away—turned off the television. *Jerry Springer* went dead without a perceptible improvement in the noise level. Not only was every television in the house blaring, so was every radio. He moved across the room to the Fisher stereo system, found the power button, and shut it down, too.

This time, there was a noticeable reduction in the clamor.

"How can you even hear yourself think?" the first officer asked.

That was the whole point. Canfield didn't want to hear himself think. He wanted to drown out every last syllable rattling around inside his head, because they didn't belong to him. Not the words. Not the voices. None of them.

While the first officer talked to him, the second went room-to-room, turning off television sets and radios, even the computer in the spare bedroom, which had been running a Bruce Springsteen CD. Each time something went off, the noise in Canfield's head grew louder.

"You been drinking, Herb?"

"Yeah, sure. A couple beers."

"We gonna find any drugs in the house?"

"No. Nothing. I don't do drugs."

"Then what's with all the racket? You got something

All the Lonely People / 96

going on between you and your neighbors? You trying to piss them off?"

"No, it's nothing like that," Canfield said. Pressure was beginning to build inside his head. He felt like he needed to sneeze, but he was afraid if he did, his eyeballs would blow out. That picture sent a shiver through him; it also made him want to laugh. "I was in the mood for some volume, that's all."

"Well, you need to get out of the mood, because if we have to come back out here again, we're gonna haul you in for disturbing the peace. Is that clear? I don't want to get another call from one of your neighbors."

The second officer emerged from the back of the house and joined them. Everything was quiet now. Canfield could hear water flowing into the refrigerator's ice maker, the occasional crackle of the house settling, a car going by outside. But most of all, he could hear the frenzied cacophony of strange voices in his head.

"If you can't live without the noise," the first officer said, "try using headphones. At least your neighbors won't be up all night."

Canfield nodded. "I'll do that."

They took their time leaving. Canfield did his best to smile through the small talk, even though the effort left the muscles in his face feeling as if someone had slugged him. More than he probably should have, he apologized for his behavior. He'd had a hard day, he said. The clamor was just an attempt to drown out the grief.

When the front door finally closed, he fell against it.

There were screams echoing inside his head, an uproar of wailing voices, of torment and anguish and desperation.

Canfield clamped his hands over his ears, barely able to find his balance amid the chaos.

When he realized the pandemonium was only getting worse, he pushed away from the door and went stumbling down the hall, looking for the headphones.

David B. Silva / 97

PART VII:
FLAKING

1

The phone call hadn't come in yet—it was still a good ten minutes away—so it wasn't the sound of the telephone that woke Chase. It wasn't the fact that he'd spent the night sleeping downstairs in the recliner again, either. In fact, he'd begun to find the old chair more comfortable than the bed he shared with Karla.

What woke Chase was the incessant itching.

He opened his eyes and glanced down at his left arm, where he had rolled the sleeve up above the elbow. On the forearm, like an infectious disease, an egg-shaped area had been scratched raw. Blood seeped from the heart of the opening, along with a clear, viscous material. Around the edges, the skin was dry and discolored. It almost appeared as if his arm was beginning to rot. Only there was no pain. Just that constant itching sensation.

Chase felt drawn to continue scratching until . . .

Until he saw the collection of blood under his fingernails and realized even in his sleep he'd been after that itch. The lesion, with its ugly gray lip, was his own damn creation. *He* had been the one who had burrowed under the surface, down into the flesh and blood. It was *his* infectious disease.

That realization got him out of the chair and upstairs to the master bathroom in a panic. He dug a small tube of Neosporin out of the middle cabinet drawer, and nearly emptied it covering the wound. He covered the salve with a gauze pad, covered the gauze pad with several layers of rolled gauze, then secured the bandaging with the help of some medical tape.

There.

Not so bad.

It still itched some, but it wasn't so bad it left him feeling out of control (although almost immediately the thought popped into his head that the eraser end of a pencil might relieve the last little bit of irritation, if he could just slip it under the edge of the bandage). Tonight, if he wore a long-sleeved shirt to bed, with the cuffs buttoned and maybe a jacket on top, that should keep him from digging around under there while he slept. A day or two without him picking at it, and maybe the wound would begin to heal.

Chase removed his sunglasses, placed them on the bathroom counter, and splashed some water on his face. With droplets running down his cheeks, over his chin, he stared at his reflection in the mirror. It was like looking at a stranger. Most mornings, he shaved, combed his hair, brushed his teeth, did all of these things face-to-face with his reflection in the mirror. But he never really looked at himself. Not past the image inside his head of how he thought he should look.

Something was wrong with his eyes.

They weren't the way he remembered them.

The pupils were dilated, of course, but that wasn't it. Nor was it the fact that his eyes were bloodshot; that came with the territory when you weren't sleeping much.

No, it was the color that was wrong. His eyes had always been hazel-blue, but they were black now. Pure black. It was like looking deep into the waters of a well. There was something dead behind these eyes, something decomposing.

They belonged behind sunglasses.

Chase slipped back into the sunglasses, dried his face with a towel, and went back downstairs to the kitchen.

All the Lonely People / 102

It was early afternoon. Sometime during the night, a new storm had come over the mountains. The sky was dark, the air heavy with moisture. It hadn't started to rain yet, but it wouldn't be long. He could smell the dampness gathering.

Chase poured himself a glass of milk, took a sip, and left it on the counter. In his mind, it felt like any other afternoon at home, with Karla off at work and Danielle at school. He'd been so preoccupied with the wound he'd opened up on his arm that he'd forgotten Danielle was in the hospital. He only remembered when he noticed her flutter tube on the kitchen table. Karla was going to raise holy hell about her leaving it lying around like that, he thought, and then he realized, as if a series of lazy synopses had suddenly ignited . . . Danielle had bigger problems than where she had left her flutter tube.

I need to call the hospital.

Chase started across the room to the phone on the wall, but it rang before he had a chance to pick it up. There was a female voice on the other end. Though it sounded familiar, several beats went by before he realized it didn't belong to Karla. It belonged to Maddie.

"I didn't know who else to call," she said softly, almost too low to understand. "Not Ben or Sam, you know, because I don't know them that well. Not really. I suppose I don't know you that well, either, but with you, it's like I feel like I kinda know you. At least I trust you."

Chase sat down at the kitchen table, the phone to his ear. He shaded his eyes. A picture of Maddie came up in his mind: curly reddish-brown hair, a little more makeup than was necessary, an enduring expression of sadness. The picture came and went in a flash. It was replaced with the image of Ben Tucker peeking over the top of a brick wall. There was a look on his face like he thought the devil was coming for him.

"I need help, Chase."

"What kind of help?"

"I need someone to tell me I'm not crazy."

David B. Silva / 103

We're all crazy.

"You aren't," Chase said.

"Really? You're really sure about that? Because it feels like I'm crazy."

"You've been losing time and forgetting things, haven't you? Your eyes can't stand the light. You can't sleep at night. You've been getting terrible headaches."

"Forgetting's the worst," she said.

Because you lose track of what's real and what isn't, Chase thought.

The conversation fell quiet.

Chase glanced down and found himself absently scratching at his dressing. He could see a faint elliptical outline of red beginning to form. He pulled his hand away. There was still no pain, just that annoying itch, but he could tell now that it wasn't going to heal as fast as he had hoped. He'd have to keep a close eye on it, probably need to change the dressing several times a day.

He moved his hand off the table and placed it in his lap.

Maddie hadn't said another word.

She's lapsed, Chase thought. *Or* I've *lapsed.*

It was hard to know which.

"Maddie? You still there?"

All the Lonely People / 104

2

The screensaver on James Cleaver's work computer said: What's the difference between a CPA and a shopping cart? Answer: A CPA holds more beverages.

Not long ago, before the current message, the screensaver had said: What's an accountant's idea of trashing his hotel room? Answer: Refusing to fill out the guest comment card. And before that: How do you tell if an accountant is an extrovert or an introvert? Answer: An extrovert looks at *your* shoes when talking to you, an introvert looks at *his* shoes when talking to you. Those, however, had cut a little too close to home for James.

But then everything seemed like it cut too close to home lately.

He was hunched forward in his junior executive chair, his eyes hidden behind a pair of sunglasses, the fingers of his right hand busy tapping out a series of computations on a Sharp desktop calculator. His jacket hung over the outside corner of the cubicle wall. The top two buttons of his white shirt were open. The knot in his tie hung loose around his neck.

Numbers marched across the calculator's digital display like little toy soldiers.

Doggedly, they advanced across one row of paper after another.

Obediently, his fingers *tap-tap-tapped* the endless series of figures as they filled his head.

He could barely keep up. The data was bleeding out of him faster than he could bring it to mind. Day after day, it had been like this. Night after night. Actuary tables. Mortgage rate payment schedules. Accumulated amortizations. Intensity drivers. Leverage ratios. Soft costs.

"James?"

He glanced over his shoulder, his fingers continuing to work madly over the calculator keys. The man standing in the entrance to the cubicle was Lawrence J. Matson, a senior partner at Evanhoe, Matson & Company. Not the Matson in the company name, but the son. James had always found the man surprisingly easygoing, considering he'd lived his entire life under the shadow of his father.

"If I could, I'd like to see you in my office."

James nodded. "Sure. Just give me a minute, will you?"

5.6 percent. 360 payments. Loan value of $278,500. What's the monthly payment?

He started to climb out of the chair, but found he couldn't take his fingers off the keypad.

$1,598.81.

He plopped down again, and used his free hand to tighten his tie. It wasn't as easy a chore as he might have imagined. Nor was it easy to reach for his suit jacket and slip into it one arm at a time while keeping the calculator humming.

5.45 percent. 180 payments. Monthly payment: $989.21. What's the loan value?

But he managed just the same.

$121,460.

He went through another run of calculations, stood, then sat down and ran through another run, then another, unable to stop himself until the phone on his desk finally interrupted. James picked it up, his fingers

All the Lonely People / 106

never missing a beat as they danced their own little flamenco across the keypad.

"Mr. Cleaver, I'm waiting."

"Sorry. On my way." If there were a way to bring the calculator with him, he would have done it. What he needed was one of those portables, without the printer, just a display screen. Something battery-powered. But that wasn't an option, not here and now at least.

James tore his fingers free from the keypad, and cold turkey, started down the aisle without looking back.

Inside his head, numbers rattled off in an endless loop. Except they were all different, all unique, each with its own traits, its own flavor.

The square root of 31,329 = 177.

5.67 % of 983,564 = 55,768.08

3x3x3x3x3x3x3x3x3x3x3 = 59,049

Lawrence Matson's office was situated in the corner of the building, at the far end of the floor, overlooking Simpson Park. The door was open. James knocked and entered, all in one motion. Matson motioned him to a chair, then sat down behind a desk that was nearly as big as the cubicle where James worked.

"How are things these days?" Matson asked.

"Fine. Things are fine."

"Really?"

"Yes. Fine."

"The reason I feel compelled to inquire, James, is because we've been worried about you lately. Your behavior's been rather . . . out of character."

17x + 32 x 9.38% = 16987

What's x?

1063.276.

"You've always been an exemplary employee. You're a hard worker. You get along great with everyone. You're self-motivated. We'd really hate to have to let you go."

Doesn't matter, James thought between the streams of numbers. *Sooner or later the numbers are going to quit adding up. Sooner or later, they're going to run out.*

Then nothing will matter.

"But lately you've seemed somewhat . . . distracted, I guess is the best way to put it. You never followed up on the Monroe account, James. That's not like you. They've requested to work with someone else or they're going to take their business elsewhere. And you still haven't finished the preliminaries on the Williams Paint account."

Doesn't matter.

Doesn't matter.

Doesn't matter.

"I was hoping you might be able to explain yourself."

Frenetically, his fingers tapped out number after number on the armrest of his chair.

360 payments.

$339,000 loan value.

Monthly payments: $2178.51.

What's the interest rate?

6.66%

666.

James Cleaver laughed.

Matson, who had been sitting with his elbows on the desk and a grave expression on his face, sank back into his leather-upholstered executive chair. He studied James closely, trying to read something in his face that apparently was unreadable. "Do me a favor, would you, James? Remove your sunglasses."

"The light hurts my eyes."

"Just humor me."

"I know what you're thinking," James said. The square root of 17,689 is 133. The square root of 443,556 is . . . 666. *Ah, there it is again!* "You're thinking I'm on something. Not true. Not true at all. Occasionally, I'll treat myself to a beer, but that's the full extent of my substance abuse. Honest to God. *That* and a cigarette after sex. But since I can't remember the last time I had sex, that hardly counts, now does it?"

Matson smiled sadly. "Okay, here's what we're going

All the Lonely People / 108

to do, James. We're going to send you home for a few weeks. Use up your vacation time, your sick leave, whatever it takes. Talk to someone. Get some help. See if you can work through whatever it is that's bothering you. When you think you're feeling better, give me a call. We'll see if we can set you up with a new client for a probationary period."

Doesn't matter.

Doesn't matter.

Doesn't matter.

Nothing mattered anymore, because soon the numbers wouldn't add up.

They would never add up again.

3

That he had known so little about Ben Tucker bothered Chase more than he would have expected. That he knew even less about Maddie Ashburn— and in fact, had never crossed paths with her, not once in eleven years, outside The Last Stop—bothered him even more.

That was about to change.

After her phone call, he knew he'd have to track her down.

First, though, Chase stopped by the hospital to see Danielle. It was the middle of the afternoon by then. The dark clouds that had been threatening all morning had finally let loose. Water was everywhere, overrunning gutters and drains, flooding intersections, collecting in pools, some the size of a small house.

In the hospital parking lot, Chase stepped into a puddle and sank all the way to the top of his sock. It was only the one foot, but even so, every other step down the hospital corridor to the elevators had been wet and noisy and unpleasant.

That calamity had been followed by the discovery that Danielle had been moved. The new room was supposed to be one floor up, across from the nurse's station. Only Danielle wasn't there. Neither was Karla for that matter. The nurse had no idea where they were, but she suggested

All the Lonely People / 110

they might have gone downstairs for x-rays.

X-rays? Why would Danielle need x-rays?

She wouldn't, would she?

Chase hung around for a good half-hour, then decided he didn't want to wait any longer. He left a note on Danielle's pillow, saying he was sorry he'd missed her and he'd call later.

Back on the road, a few blocks away, he spotted a phone booth at a gas station. More important, he spotted a phone booth that still had a phone book. He stopped to look up Maddie's address, wrote it down on a scrap of paper from out of the glove compartment, and climbed back into the car.

Maddie Ashburn, 387 Country Rock Lane #282.

Chase assumed the number at the end indicated an apartment building. But once he tracked down the street, he realized he'd been wrong. It wasn't an apartment building; it was a mobile home park. He couldn't remember Maddie ever mentioning that she lived in a mobile home.

The park was called Riverside Estates.

Maddie's place was at the end of a nub, off a narrow one-lane road that circled the entire park. It was a single-wide, with an awning over the entrance that extended another twenty feet and doubled as a carport. Out front, she had hidden a pair of propane tanks behind a semicircle of potted adenophora. Light beige curtains covered the main window. A white-rock garden with a variety of cactus plants separated her space from the neighbors.

There was no car in the carport.

Chase parked and waited for the latest downpour to pass before he got out. Then he climbed the steps to the small porch, where more potted plants lined the entrance.

The front door was made of metal. When he knocked it made a dull, hollow sound that traveled down the outside wall in both directions.

No one answered.

Chase cupped his hands around his face and peered in

David B. Silva / 111

through the window. The lights were off. There was no movement. No sound. He could see a small television set off to the left, some dirty dishes on the kitchen counter to the right. And the telephone receiver . . .

"She's not home."

He glanced up in the direction of the voice to find a woman standing at the edge of the awning. She appeared close to Maddie's age, a little heavier. Definitely rounder in the face. Her complexion was dark, her hair black. She wiped her hands on a dirty apron, then brushed a tuft of damp hair away from her face.

"Who are you?" she asked.

"Chase Hanford."

"Who the hell is Chase Hanford?"

"I'm a friend of Maddie's. I own a little place called The Last Stop. Out on the edge of town, off Coyote Road. Maddie's a regular there."

"Well, like I said, she's not home."

"You know where she might be?"

"She left a couple hours ago. Didn't say where she was going." The woman moved forward a few steps, under the overhang of the awning, where she was out of the drizzle. She wiped her hands on the apron again, and used the sleeve of her sweatshirt to wipe the sheen of water from her face. "She hasn't been herself lately."

Who has *she been*? Chase was tempted to ask.

"How so?"

"Been upset a lot. Heard her crying some the last couple days. That's not like her. Most the time, she's pretty quiet, stays to herself, doesn't bother no one. This morning, though . . . Christ, this morning she was running around that place, one end to the other, screaming bloody murder." The woman glanced up and waved as an old Chevy Impala slowly went by with a young woman driving and two children in the back seat. "Called over, 'cause I thought maybe someone had broke in or something. You never know. You ain't safe nowhere these days. But Maddie answered and she said she was okay. Said she

All the Lonely People / 112

was dealing with a migraine and it was just about driving her out of her gourd."

"You believe her?"

"No reason not to."

"She say anything else?"

"Nah, that was about the whole of it."

"Uh-huh." Chase glanced down and realized he'd been scratching at his bandage again. He had already changed the dressing twice, and though it still itched at least the bleeding had stopped. "No idea where she might have gone, huh?"

"Sometimes she does some volunteer work down at the Y."

"The YMCA?"

"The YWCA. South Market Street."

4

Danielle was upstairs in Room 422, watching a rerun of Home Improvement and picking at her hospital dinner. Her color had improved dramatically since she'd been admitted, and her temperature had settled in between 99 and 100 degrees, down from a high of 102. She was doing better than expected, the doctor said. She was still a day or two away from being ready to go home, mainly because her heart rate was a bit high, but overall, things were looking good.

An enormous relief for Karla, who was downstairs now, in the cafeteria, picking at her own plate of food and talking to Chase on the cell phone.

"She was disappointed she missed you," Karla said.

"I hung around for nearly an hour. Where were you?"

"We went down to the cafeteria for lunch." Karla took a bite out of a pastrami sandwich and wiped a dab of mustard from the corner of her mouth. She wasn't really hungry—like Chase, she'd always found it difficult to eat when she was under stress—but it was nice to get out of that hospital room and into a different environment for a few minutes. "Why don't you give her a call? She'll be excited to hear from you."

"I'll do that. As soon as things aren't so crazy here."

"Busy night?"

"Yeah. I've got one of the regulars covering for me. I

needed to call you and make sure everything was all right."

"She's been an angel," Karla said. For a moment, she suspected Chase might be lying to her. He didn't often call from the bar, but when he did, she could usually hear the jukebox or the ballgame in the background, and always the clamor of voices. She closed her eyes, listened, and couldn't detect any background noise at all. Of course, if he had someone covering for him, he was probably in the office with the door shut. "The doctor says we'll probably be able to go home in a couple of days."

"That's great," Chase said, his voice strangely remote.

"Danielle's happy. That's for sure."

"Bet she is."

I missed it, Karla thought out of the blue. It hit her all at once, like a strike of lightning, and she *knew*. She simply *knew*. The gulf between them had grown so wide they had quit trying to cross it. She stood on one side, Chase on the other, and between them they were scarcely aware of each other. Strangers passing in the night. It had never seemed so obvious to her as it did at this moment.

"I better let you get back to the bar before they drink you dry," Karla said.

Chase laughed politely. "They will, too."

"Don't forget to call Danielle."

"I won't."

But she knew he'd forget. The gulf stood between Chase and Danielle, too.

Karla hung up, surprised at how numb she felt. That was what happened, she supposed, once the gulf between two people began to grow. They quit feeling. No love, no hate. Just a tolerable degree of indifference. How come she hadn't seen it before, she wondered.

Too busy to notice. Too busy with the day-to-day. Just like your husband.

Karla put the cell phone aside and picked up her

David B. Silva / 115

sandwich. She was surprised to notice her hands were trembling. When the phone rang again, she was equally surprised at the instant tightness in her chest. Somewhere at the back of her mind, she hoped it was Chase calling her back to prove her wrong . . . there really was no gulf between them.

But the call was from her sister, Luanne. They had been playing phone tag most of the day, Karla leaving messages on her sister's machine at the house, and Luanne leaving voice mail on Karla's cell phone.

In between bites from her pastrami sandwich, Karla filled her sister in on all the latest. Danielle was doing great. The doctor was pleased with her progress, and they'd probably be going home again in a couple of days. Luanne offered to drive over from Reno, where she and her husband lived in a mobile home on ten acres of sand and cactus. She could help out for a week or two, she said, Richard wouldn't mind. But Karla assured her it wasn't necessary.

"Everything's under control," Karla insisted, and that seemed to open the door.

"Everything?"

"You know what I mean."

"So, tell me, has he visited?"

"Of course," Karla said. "He was down here last night, and again early this afternoon."

"Really?"

"You make him sound horrible. I should know better than to say anything to you. I mentioned it *once*. That's all, just *once*. Now every time you call you make it sound like he hates Danielle. That's not what I said, and it's not the way it is. Sometimes, he's just a little distant from her, that's all. It's not like they don't get along." Karla snuck a bite of her sandwich, and washed it down with some Lipton ice tea, thinking: *most of the time, they get along better than Danielle and I do.*

"Sorry. I won't bring it up again."

"Good."

All the Lonely People / 116

"So things are going good?"

Karla paused. "He hasn't been sleeping well lately. Actually, he's been acting a little . . . *strange*."

"Strange . . . how?"

"I don't know. He's been absentminded a lot. You know, forgetting things, zoning out. I thought it was because he couldn't sleep, but . . . sometimes when we're talking, this blank stare comes over him and it's like he's not even there."

Luanne laughed. "Every man does that when his wife's talking."

"And he's been wearing these sunglasses all the time. Not just outside during the day . . . but literally all the time." Karla gave up on the idea of finishing her sandwich. She dropped it onto the paper plate. "At first, I thought maybe he was having an affair, but now I'm starting to wonder if he's drinking again."

"Have you asked him?"

"He said he wasn't. Said things down at the bar were a little stressed right now, and he hadn't been sleeping that well, and it was just catching up to him, that's all."

"You believe him?"

"I don't know," Karla said. She combed a hand through her hair and sat back in the chair. There had been half-a-dozen people in the cafeteria when she'd arrived, but they were gone now, all but one man on the other side of the room, who was reading a paperback book. "You know, I don't think I want to talk about this right now. Maybe after Danielle comes home again, but for right now I just don't want to have to deal with it. If he's drinking again . . . I don't know. If he's drinking again, then I guess we've got bigger problems than I thought."

David B. Silva / 117

5

The Young Women's Christian Association was housed in the same complex as the Young Men's Christian Association. They were situated on opposite ends, separated by basketball courts, locker rooms, and a swimming pool.

Inside the front entrance, Chase stopped at the reception desk and was directed from there to a small office at the back of the facility where he was greeted by a woman in her late sixties.

"I was wondering if I could speak to whoever's in charge of your volunteer program."

"Looking to donate some time?" the woman asked. She wore a kind, friendly smile that almost veiled the fact that when she spoke, the loose skin around her thin neck jiggled like Jell-O.

"Actually, I'm looking for a woman by the name of Maddie Ashburn. I was told she did some volunteer work here."

The smile wavered momentarily, then disappeared from the woman's face altogether, replaced by a gravity Chase had rarely seen on another person's face. She let out a long breath. Her eyes darkened. She seemed to grow an inch or two as she adjusted her position in the chair. "Are you a relative of Miss Ashburn's?"

"Just a friend."

All the Lonely People / 118

"I see." The woman stood and worked her way around the desk in a slow, deliberate movement that suggested she might have an arthritic knee. Pinned to her yellow blouse, she wore a name tag. It read: Agnes Livingston. "Maybe you can help. We've been trying to locate a relative, but the family references in her file, well, they seem to be a bit out of date."

Trying to reach her why?

Chase followed the elderly woman out of the room, feeling like he was ten-years-old again, following the teacher to the principal's office. They moved down a long hall toward the far end of the building. On both sides, the walls were painted a soothing light green, with yellow and white horizontal stripes that made him think of the hospital. He wondered if the same company had painted both places, and then he wondered how Danielle was doing.

"Maddie came in about an hour ago, feeling . . . confused. At first, I thought she might need medical attention, but she insisted she just needed to hide. That was what she said: she needed to hide. I didn't ask what she was hiding from, but I called the Director and explained the situation. She said she'd see if she could get someone down here to talk with Maddie. That's what I've been waiting on. For a bit there, when you first arrived, I thought maybe Carolyn wasn't available."

"Who's Carolyn?"

"Dr. Carolyn Maynard. She's the family therapist who works with some of our clients." Agnes Livingston was a tiny woman. Even at a leisurely pace her arms swung in a huge pendulum-like arc, working nearly as hard as her legs.

At the end of the hall, they arrived at a door with a gold-and-black placard that said: Staff Lounge.

"We came close to calling the police initially, because she seemed so agitated. We didn't want her hurting herself." The woman cupped her hand around the doorknob, but she didn't open the door. Instead, she

David B. Silva / 119

went on talking. "Maddie's been volunteering here for longer than I can remember. She's never been very social, always been on the quiet side, but she's a hard worker. When she says she'll be here, she'll be here. You can't always count on that from a volunteer. So many of them have the idea that since they're giving their time they can come and go as they please. Not Maddie. She's been a gem. We really treasure her."

Chase motioned toward the door. "You sure it's all right? I don't want to upset her."

"Dr. Maynard should be along shortly. I don't see any reason why she'd object to Maddie spending some time with a friend."

Agnes Livingston opened the door. "Maddie? There's someone here to see you."

The room was larger than Chase had expected. There were two huge picture windows along the outside wall, draped in blinds, the slats open wide enough that he could see his own car in the parking lot out back. On one side were two vending machines, one for soft drinks, the other for snacks. Between them, set up on a small table, was half-a-pot of coffee keeping warm in a Mr. Coffee maker. Maddie was sitting on the opposite side of the room, at one end of a sofa, a pillow pulled into her lap. Her hair was ratted and wild. There were dark circles under her eyes. Her coloring was pasty, almost ghost-like.

"Hi, Maddie."

She glanced at him out of the corner of her eye.

"I'll be down the hall if you need anything," Agnes Livingston said.

The door closed behind her as she left.

An uneasy silence fell over the room.

Chase leaned against the wall, his hands tucked behind his back while he tried to find something to say. He'd expected to find Maddie in much the same shape as he'd found Ben: rattled, frightened, but also angry and resilient. Instead, she looked like a little girl who had

All the Lonely People / 120

been lost in the wilderness for several days. Fear had already taken her. In her place, it had left a hollow shell of the woman she had been.

"Whenever I touch anything, my skin vibrates," Maddie said. "You know . . . *tingles*? It's like two surfaces mixing. There's no sense of separateness, no . . . solidness."

"Ben Tucker's been having problems, too."

She raised her head. A brief expression of recognition or hope or understanding, Chase wasn't sure which, crossed her face.

"Me, too," Chase said. "Not as bad, though. Not like you."

There was a reason for that. It was the only reason he'd been able to come up with that made any sense. Chase had been the only person in the bar who hadn't looked directly into the box that night. It was as if he'd been able to avoid the full impact of the light.

"My eyes are sensitive to light," Chase said. "I'm having trouble sleeping. I've been losing time."

Maddie nodded, and began to rock back and forth. She'd been holding onto the pillow as if it were a life preserver and the waters were rising. Because of that, Chase hadn't noticed what she was wearing. It was a man's suit, black, with a white dress shirt and a black-and-gray striped tie that looked as if it had been tied by someone who didn't know what she was doing. There was a pair of shiny black dress shoes on her feet, four sizes too large, the laces undone. Underneath the shoes, Maddie wore a pair of white socks.

"Time?" she said. Her voice was raw. Chase thought back to the neighbor who had told him Maddie had been screaming bloody murder all morning. "I'm losing memories. I think they come and steal them at night when it's dark and I can't keep my eyes open."

He didn't want to ask, because he didn't want to know, but he couldn't *not* ask, either. "Who, Maddie? Who comes at night?"

David B. Silva / 121

"The lost shadows."

A shiver passed through him. This was something new, something he hadn't experienced for himself. Ben Tucker had alluded to things getting worse, though, hadn't he? Chase pressed back against the wall again, his hands still tucked behind him in a position that somehow made him feel more under control. He wondered how much worse things could possibly get?

"What do they look like?"

Maddie looked up at him, then glanced to his right, and nodded. "Like that. Like a black mist."

There was nothing there. A line of gray, four-drawer filing cabinets stood shoulder-to-shoulder against the wall, but that was it. That, and a photograph of a building in the early stages of construction. Chase assumed it was a photo of this same complex.

"Sitting on the cabinets," Maddie said.

There was nothing sitting on the cabinets.

"Can't see it, can you?"

"No," Chase said, honestly wishing he could.

"You will. Eventually."

"What is it?"

"A straggler."

A *straggler*, Chase thought. It sounded like a word he might have used to describe himself, or maybe Ben Tucker, or even Maddie.

The pillow slipped out of her lap and fell to the floor. Maddie bent over to retrieve it. She snatched it back with surprising speed, but not before Chase had caught a glimpse of what it had been concealing. Under the pillow, Maddie was hiding something that looked like a coffee table book.

"What have you got there?"

"Nothing."

"Looked like a book to me," Chase said.

"It's not." She scooted deeper into the corner of the sofa, her rocking motion suddenly stilled. Her arms tightened around the pillow as if it were her child and she

All the Lonely People / 122

were protecting it. "It's mine."

"I can see that. What is it?"

Maddie looked down at whatever she was concealing, then looked up at Chase, debating if she should or if she shouldn't. "If I show you, you have to give it back."

"Of course." Chase held out his hand. The room around him began to turn hazy and out of focus around the edges. Air emptied from his lungs. His eyes grew heavy. He wasn't going to be here much longer. Another *lapse* was on its way. When it arrived, he was going to drift away to the land of nothingness for a time.

"Promise?" Maddie asked.

"Promise."

It wasn't a book; it was a photograph album. With both hands, Maddie brought it out from beneath the pillow and handed it to him. Embossed across the cover were the words: The Life And Times of Maddie Ashburn.

"My father gave it to me for my thirteenth birthday."

Chase could almost feel the weight slipping through his hands. It was as if he were no longer solid, as if the album had nothing to prevent it from dropping to the floor. Hadn't Maddie said something about not feeling solid? Was *this* what she'd meant? This . . . strange lightness of matter? This . . . ghostliness?

"The pictures, they help me hold onto my memories," Maddie said. "If I lose them . . . "

"Your father . . . " Chase asked. The rest of the thought slipped away from him, and for a moment he was certain it was lost forever. His mind went blank. He could feel himself drifting aimlessly. Out of focus. Groggy. Then suddenly the thought finished itself: "Those his clothes you're wearing?"

Maddie said something back, but Chase wasn't sure what it was.

He closed his eyes.

A noise rose up from behind him. It sounded like the door opening.

Somewhere in his thoughts, he wondered if another

David B. Silva / 123

straggler had entered the room.

That brought a chuckle. *First you gotta see the one sitting on the filing cabinets, then you can start worrying about the one coming through the door.* It all seemed absurdly amusing, like things sometimes did in the old days when he'd get drunk and fall off the bar stool. Two *stragglers*! Not one, but two!

Then Chase let his head loll back against the wall and he promptly faded away.

PART VIII:
NOTES TO REMEMBER BY

1

Uncle Charlie's was a step back in time.

Just the kind of place the old man had been looking for.

He parked the car at the outer edges of the lot, where the pavement had been replaced by weeds and dirt. If you drove by and gave a cursory glance at the place, you'd assume it had probably been closed for quite some time. But there were lights in the windows (Miller Genuine Draft, Budweiser, Heineken), and three cars were parked in front of the hitching posts.

He poured himself a cup of hot coffee from a Thermos bottle, and watched as another customer drove up, parked, got out and went inside. Tendrils of heat rose from the cup. He blew across the liquid surface, then took a sip. Not great, but better than nothing. At least it helped warm his bones. He screwed the cap back onto the Thermos bottle and placed the Thermos on the seat, next to the cardboard box.

There were seven people inside now.

Plenty.

Another sip of coffee.

His hands were shaking, not as severely as last time, but bad enough that he had to use them both to keep the coffee from spilling over the lip of the cup. Maybe this was how it would always be. Maybe it was never going to

David B. Silva / 127

get any easier.

Down the slippery slope we slide . . .

The sun dropped behind a distant mountain and the sky seemed to darken instantly. A yard light at each end of the building, mounted on the roof of the overhang, kicked on. The dirt and gravel lot fell into a rugged landscape of shadow and light, looking something like the surface of the moon, only seedier, less friendly.

The old man finished his coffee. He placed the cup on the seat, next to the Thermos, and climbed out of the car. He went around to the passenger's side, opened the door, and brought out the cardboard box. There was no way to be certain, but he thought it felt heavier than last time.

It had been years since the place had been painted. Dark and stained by age, the pine siding had begun to pull away from the framing. The wood plank porch, which ran the full length of the building, was soft under the old man's steps. The overhang sagged from the weight of too many heavy winters.

He stopped and balanced the weight of the cardboard box before entering.

A bell rang overhead as the door swung open.

The faces of strangers glanced up to see if he was someone they knew. He wasn't. He'd never been here before. Never to Uncle Charlie's. He'd passed through the town a time or two, when he still had his territory and he was at the top of his game. Those were the years when he'd been winning paid vacations and new cars for being the company's top salesman. They seemed like someone else's memories now.

The old man waded through the blanket of sawdust and peanut shells on the floor to the nearest stool at the bar. He removed his hat, his coat, dropped them on the stool next to him, then placed the cardboard box on the counter where everyone could see it.

"What can I get for you?" The bartender was a young man in his late twenties. His face was pockmarked above a light beard that had less than a week's growth. There

All the Lonely People / 128

was a skull-and-crossbones earring in his left ear. His black hair was shoulder-length and banded in a ponytail. He was not someone you would want to bump into late at night.

Maybe that will make this easier.

"A draft should do the trick." The old man pulled a five spot out of his wallet and set it on the counter. When the beer arrived, he slid the bill across the smooth, lacquered surface.

"Thanks."

"Thanks for the beer."

Around the room, curiosity was already stirring. One of the first rules of good salesmanship: Never sell the customer. Let the customer sell himself.

To do that, first you had to get them curious.

2

It had taken nearly as long to get released from the hospital as their stay had been.

Okay, that was an exaggeration, but it was a *slight* exaggeration. Between the forms, the prescriptions they had to wait on, and the last minute instructions that came down from the doctor to the nurse, the process had taken several hours.

Karla and Danielle left the hospital exhausted and eager to get home. First, they had to stop somewhere to fill the prescriptions. Then Karla wasn't sure if there was any food in the house, so they stopped at Safeway to pick up groceries.

Those two chores took better than an hour.

It was sneaking up on midnight, by the time they came through the door between the garage and the laundry room,

"I'm going to bed," Danielle said, her eyes dull and barely open.

"'Night, honey. You can sleep in tomorrow if you'd like."

"What about school?"

"One more day won't hurt."

Danielle nodded and yawned. She gave Karla a kiss on the cheek, then shuffled off toward the stairway.

Karla dropped the bag of groceries on the kitchen

All the Lonely People / 130

counter. There was a muscle in her lower back that had tightened up. She stretched, and thought how nice it was going to be to sleep in her own bed again.

The sink was full of dirty dishes. Some were left from breakfast the day Danielle had gone into the hospital. They had been running late that morning, and Karla remembered feeling guilty about it as she was stacking them in the sink. The rest belonged to Chase.

At least he's been eating, she thought.

She placed the lettuce and tomatoes in the crisper, closed the refrigerator door and found herself staring at the stack of dishes again. *Maybe he hasn't.* In typical fashion, Chase had dumped his dishes in the sink without scraping them first. There was a sandwich on the top that looked as if it hadn't been touched. Under that, a leftover tuna casserole and a salad that had gone bad. Maybe he wasn't eating at all.

I oughta dump the whole mess in a bag, take it down to the bar, and leave it on the counter, Karla thought. It was demanding enough trying to keep after Danielle all the time, she didn't need the added burden of trying to keep after a little boy, too.

She dug around the bottom of the shopping bag and brought out a package of hamburger (7% fat), a couple onions, and some Ranch-style dressing. There was spaghetti in the pantry, along with Lipton Onion Soup Mix. That should be enough for spaghetti and meatballs, plus a green salad for dinner tomorrow night. For breakfast . . .

Karla glanced up. Danielle was standing in the kitchen doorway. "Thought you were going to bed?"

"There's something you need to see."

"I'm almost done here."

"You need to see it now," Danielle said.

3

Chase opened his eyes and for several long seconds—because there was nothing but darkness—he thought it had finally happened . . . he had died.

Gradually, though, as his eyes adjusted, he was able to make out the ridge of a mountain cutting a jagged line across the night sky. He saw this through the windshield of the car. Then he became aware of his hands wrapped around the steering wheel, the cool air all around him, the sound of crickets outside, the twinkle of stars stepping out of the darkness.

The *lapses* were getting longer.

He was venturing farther.

The car wasn't moving. It was parked, thank God. Below the skyline, the darkness was nearly impenetrable. Chase glanced out the side windows, then out the back, looking for a sign of civilization, maybe a glow of city lights in the distance or the outside lights of a nearby farm house.

Nothing.

It was like waking up to discover you're the last person on Earth.

He had no idea where he was, or even how he'd gotten here.

After some blind fumbling, he discovered the keys still

in the ignition. Chase started the engine. "The House of The Rising Sun" by The Animals came up on the radio. Listening to that, he wondered what time it was and how much longer it would be before sunrise.

The dashboard lights were off, as were the headlights. He flipped them on, thinking either he'd had the presence of mind to turn them off after he'd parked, or he'd been sitting out here since sometime before nightfall.

It was 12:34, according to the digital clock.

The headlights fell across the rocky terrain of a dirt road. There didn't appear to be any tire tracks in front of him. On both sides, the landscape appeared to be barren, except for an occasional young manzanita bush or an old tree stump. This had been the end of the journey. To find his way back, he needed to turn around and follow the tire tracks to the first paved road.

Chase backed up until the rear end of the car started to climb the landscape. Then he stopped, shifted gears, and swung the car around. Ahead of him now, for the first time he could see tire tracks in the soft dirt. The sight brought an instant sense of relief.

At least he had way out.

4

Standing in the kitchen doorway, Danielle's arms were wrapped tight around her body as if she were trying to hold herself together. Her eyes were large and animated, her face ashen, and her breathing slightly labored, though sometimes it was difficult to tell. She looked nearly as bad as she had the day she'd gone into the hospital.

"What's the matter, honey?"

"Mom, please."

"Okay, okay, I'm coming." Karla left the hamburger on the kitchen counter. There was something in the tone of Danielle's voice that scared her. As she followed her daughter upstairs, she began to understand what it was. She was scared because Danielle was scared.

"This is so weird," Danielle said gravely. A chill passed through Karla. They stopped at the top of the stairs. Danielle motioned across the hall to her room. "I don't want to go in there again."

Karla looked from Danielle to the bedroom door and back to Danielle again, trying to find a reason why her daughter would be so upset. She crossed the hallway and stopped at the door, taking one more opportunity to look back at Danielle for a clue about what she might find on the other side of the door.

Danielle shuddered.

All the Lonely People / 134

Karla placed her palm against the door and pushed.

Lazily, the door swung open.

When Karla could finally see through the opening, she couldn't believe her eyes.

"You think someone's stalking me?" Danielle asked.

Karla couldn't find the words. She mumbled something that even she didn't understand, but *yes*, she thought, *at first glance it looks like someone's stalking you.*

The walls were papered with photographs of Danielle. There were birth photos, her first day at kindergarten, the family camping trip to Yosemite three years ago. In place of the Aaron Carter poster next to her bed, there was a blow up of her school picture from the second grade, when she'd had a lazy eye and the doctor insisted she wear a patch. Polaroids. 35mm shots. Digital photos that had been run through a color printer and enlarged. A picture of last year's birthday party. A shot of Danielle wearing a new blouse she'd saved up and bought with her own money.

Every last inch of the walls, floor to ceiling, was covered.

Outlets were papered over.

Vents.

This wasn't a prank. There was something obsessive about this. Fanatical.

"Who would want to do this to me?" Danielle asked from the hallway.

"I don't know," Karla said honestly. She *didn't* know, not for certain, but she had an idea.

"So what do we do now? Call the police?"

"Not yet." Karla backed out of the room, almost mesmerized by the gallery. Someone had built a shrine to her daughter, and he had done it in her daughter's room. " I want to check something downstairs first. I'll be right back, all right? You going to be okay?"

Danielle nodded, and sat down on the top stair. Her face was long, her head down. She fidgeted with the

David B. Silva / 135

hospital tag still wrapped around her wrist, looking like a little girl lost in the crowd.

"Promise. I won't be long."

Karla went downstairs to the living room. They had always kept the family photos in the bottom drawer of the bookshelves, beneath the set of Encyclopedia Britannica, which no one had opened in nearly five years because it was more fun on the Internet. She sat on the floor and sorted through the drawer, through the albums and the negatives and the piles of photographs that had come back from the developer and gone straight in here without a glance. Most of the pictures they took were of Danielle, and most of those were missing.

They were upstairs in Danielle's room, on the walls.

My God, if this was Chase . . .

Who else could it have been? Apparently, nothing else in the house had been disturbed. Nothing taken. Nothing damaged. Who else had access? Who else knew where they kept their photos? Who else . . .

Karla stopped herself there. Chase hadn't been himself lately. She wasn't sure what he was going through, if it was a physical problem or an emotional one, but he'd been unusually withdrawn and distant. She'd tried to tell him at the hospital that he needed to see someone.

She climbed the stairs much slower than she had come down them, the burden already weighing on her. What was she was going to say to Danielle?

"Did you call the cops?"

"No, honey." Karla sat down on the top step, next to her daughter. Lovingly, she combed her fingers through Danielle's hair, wishing she had the words to make this easy. "I don't think the photographs were meant to upset you."

"What do you mean?"

"I don't think he was trying to scare you or anything like that. I think he was just . . . "

Danielle, who had been toying with her hospital tag,

All the Lonely People / 136

looked up. There had been times during her stay at the hospital when she had looked so delicate, so helpless that it had frightened Karla. Her mouth was straight now, her brows relaxed, and she looked strong again, certainly stronger than Karla felt. "It was Dad, wasn't it?"

Nothing gets by you, does it? Karla thought, surprised.

"He's been under a lot of stress," she said softly. "He hasn't been sleeping, and I think it caught up with him."

"Is he going to be all right?"

"We'll just have to make sure of that, won't we?"

Danielle nodded, her face a sketch in sadness. "He's not . . . like . . . you know . . . like crazy or anything, is he?"

"I don't think it's that bad."

"What if it is?"

"Then we'll get him some help," Karla said. She took Danielle's hand, gave it a reassuring squeeze, and did her best to put on a smile. "Hey, we're always there for each other in this family. Okay? That's what being a family is all about. Your father and I were there for you when you were in the hospital, and we'll be there for him."

Danielle nodded uncertainly. "You really think he's going to be all right?"

"I don't know, honey," Karla said. The words came out much colder than she intended and she didn't like the fact that she had let that happen. The truth was . . . she didn't know what was wrong with Chase, and she didn't know if he would be all right again or not. If he was drinking again, well, that was something no one controlled but him. "We'll just have to give it some time and see how it goes."

"What am I supposed to say to him next time I see him?"

"Just talk to him like you always do."

"Yeah, but what about my room?"

"It might be better if you don't mention it," Karla said. She ran her hand across her daughter's back, wishing she had the power to make everything better. "And tomorrow we'll redecorate."

"Really?"

"Promise."

"Good. Because I think I'd go crazy if I had to spend a night in there. It's like staring at yourself all the time. It's weird. Definitely weird." Danielle tugged on the hospital tag on her wrist, then pointed it out to Karla. "Can we cut this thing off?"

5

A mile-and-a-half down the road, Chase finally realized he'd been in these foothills before.

This was where he used to bring Karla when they were dating. It was away from the city lights, where the sky was darker, the stars brighter. They used to lie next to each other on the hood of the car and count the shooting stars. The crickets would be the only sound in the night. They made love on a sleeping bag on the ground on their fourth date. Chase was amazed he could still remember. So many of his other memories were beginning to slip away.

The dirt road followed the ridge of a hill.

Gradually, the vegetation grew thicker. Pine trees began to appear. The road leveled out, most of the ruts disappeared. A ditch with standing water materialized on the north side, dug to handle the winter runoff no doubt. This was an old logging road. At one time, it likely went back into the mountains for miles. But they'd done clear-cutting back here, or there had been a fire or something. That was why the terrain behind him had been so barren.

Eventually, the dirt road turned to gravel and the gravel turned to pavement. The transition was nearly transparent. It wasn't long before Chase came upon the first crossroad with a street sign.

Old Rooster Ridge.

The name was unfamiliar, so he kept on the same road until it finally came up to a stop sign at a "T" junction. To his left, far off in the distance, he could see the faint twinkle of city lights in the valley. He turned left and wound along the edge of the hills as the elevation continued to drop.

Thirteen miles further down the road, the city lights grew brighter. Farm houses began to appear, set back from the road, beneath the trees and along the base of the foothills. Chase crossed a bridge, then came up to the first illuminated intersection. He knew this place. There was an In and Out Market on one corner, Newberry's Printing across the street. The other two lots were vacant, but that didn't matter. All that mattered was that he knew this place.

He turned left onto Hawthorne Road, where a small business district was lined with streetlights. This was when, little by little, out of the corner of his eye, Chase became aware of the notes. He caught a glimpse of them, then looked closer and the sight sent a dreadful chill through him.

"Christ!"

The car swerved to the right. Chase hit the brakes. The front right tire rolled up against the curb, and Chase nearly fell out of the driver's side door trying to escape. It wasn't that he'd never seen notes before, hell his desk at the office was littered with them, but these notes . . . *these* notes had appeared out of nowhere.

Chase paced at the side of the road, his words fogging the air. "This is getting crazy, man. Way too crazy. I can't handle this shit. Not like this. Not this hocus pocus, out of nowhere shit."

A lazy drizzle of rain fell nearly unnoticed around him.

They were just notes. Thoughts on paper. That was all.

Yeah, but they weren't there a moment ago.

His pacing took him around to the other side of the

All the Lonely People / 140

car. He stopped and gaze in through the window. The notes—there were maybe as many as fifteen, all Post-It notes, plastered across the passenger side dashboard, the door, the seat—they had all been written in thick, black, felt-tip pen. And the handwriting was his.

When? When had he done that?

They hadn't been there out on the old dirt road, he was certain of that.

Was he starting to lose not just time, but time inside of time? Was that it? Not just the next hour, but ten minutes inside the hour? Was that even possible?

There was one note in particular that caught his eye. It was plastered to the dashboard, the cast of the streetlight falling across it like a beacon. It was short and to the point: Danielle is in the hospital.

When had that happened? Chase wondered.

While you were busy losing time. Or losing your mind. Because they're one and the same, aren't they?

He sat on the concrete curb, next to the entrance to Kathy's Kakes, and pulled out his cell phone.

6

Except for security lights in the parking lot and on the first three floors, the Evanhoe, Matson & Company building was a dark husk that blended nearly invisibly into the night.

James Cleaver popped the trunk of his car, climbed out, and went around to the rear for the gun, the tire iron, and a duffle bag of supplies. He used the remote to lock the car doors, then headed for the back of the building, beyond the dumpsters full of shredded papers, where there was a maintenance entrance.

The door was rather nondescript. White. The words Emergency Exit Only painted in red at eye level. He was aware of the fact that it was rigged to the alarm system, but there were some things you had no control over—the list seemed to be growing exponentially—and you just had to deal with them the best you could.

It wasn't just the alarm system that was beyond his control, the numbers had quit adding up, too.

$368 \times 3 = 9189$.

The square root of 5625 was 444.

They'd gone insane, like he'd always feared they would.

The whole world had gone insane.

If he didn't put a stop to it . . .

James broke off the door handle using the tire iron. It

All the Lonely People / 142

bounced off the ground and rolled under the nearest dumpster. Pieces of the mechanism got caught inside the workings, but it wasn't long before he had them out and the door popped open.

Instantly, the alarm went off.

James picked up the duffle bag, and raised the gun. It was the best gun he could come up with under the circumstances. It was called a combustion potato gun, or a spud gun, or more commonly, a potato cannon. He'd never heard of such a thing before he came across it on the Internet while looking for a way to use a potato as a silencer (something he'd heard about on a news broadcast).

The gun was made of PVC pipe, a cleanout (with a cap, like you'd use for your septic system), an electric barbecue sparker, and a few other little goodies, all of which he'd picked up at Timber's Hardware. It was big and bulky, and it didn't shoot bullets. It shot potatoes. Which was better than fine for his purposes. He didn't want to kill anyone. He just wanted to put an end to the numbers now that they were beginning to lie to him.

He made his way down the hall, with the alarm following behind him now, to the reception area at the front of the building. The elevators were set in a small alcove off the lobby, three that serviced all six floors, an express that went to the executive floor at the top.

James pressed the up button. Barely audible above the sound of the alarm, the bell rang and the door to the second elevator opened. He entered, dropped the duffle bag on the floor and pressed 2.

Of course 2 might take him to 5.

Or to 3.

There was no way to be certain now that the numbers couldn't be trusted.

But it didn't matter. Even random numbers would eventually cover the entire building.

When the elevator door opened, he picked up the bag and stepped across the threshold. This was the second floor. He recognized the first desk, which belonged to Harriett Mollner, one of the few people at Evanhoe, Matson & Company he trusted.

But he didn't trust her computer.

Or her calculator.

They *couldn't* be trusted.

James dropped the duffle bag to the floor, and dug out a potato. He jammed it into the barrel of the gun, pulled the wood dowel free from the side of the barrel (where he'd attached it using Velcro; he was quite pleased with himself for that bit of innovation), and tapped the potato down to the base of the PVC barrel. Then he opened the cap on the end of the combustion chamber, and using the torch on a small propane tank—which he'd brought in the bag—filled the chamber with gas. He capped the chamber, raised the barrel and pointed it at Harriett Mollner's computer.

James Cleaver braced himself. "You lie, you die."

He pushed the button to the barbecue sparker.

Boom!

The kick not only shocked him, it knocked him backwards and sent him stumbling over the duffle bag. Seconds before computer parts and strips of paper began to rain down around him, he hit the floor on his elbows. The computer, the monitor, the entire desktop was in shambles. Shreds of potato flesh were embedded in the cubicle divider. Smoke wafted from the end of the PVC barrel.

James sat up laughing.

In the distance, barely audible beneath the sound of the continuing alarm, he could hear the wail of sirens as they began to converge on the building.

He climbed back to his feet, and dusted himself off. Then he dragged the bag and the gun down the aisle to the next cubicle. He loaded another potato, filled the combustion chamber with another shot of propane, and took aim.

In the end, the numbers were going to win.

All the Lonely People / 144

They had to. They were everywhere. You couldn't escape them.

But at least he wasn't going to make it easy.

James Cleaver fired off another shot.

7

The hospital records showed that Danielle had been released hours earlier. Chase found incredible relief in that news. She couldn't be too bad off if they'd released her. Under the streetlight, he stretched his legs, tried to find a comfortable position on the curb, and dialed home.

Karla answered. She moaned something incoherent, sounding barely conscious. As soon as she heard his voice, though, she seemed to come fully awake. "Chase? Do you have any idea how much you scared your daughter tonight? She thought someone was stalking her, that's how scared she was. She wanted me to call the police."

"Is she all right?"

"She wouldn't sleep in her own room. She's sleeping with me tonight."

Chase closed his eyes. Words were such strange things. Different meanings. Different spellings. A little nuance meant one thing, another nuance meant something else. They all sounded so foreign to him. He understood the gist of them, but they all sounded so foreign.

"Is she all right?"

"She's fine," Karla said.

"Thank God."

"How could you do that to her? That's what I don't

get. What were you thinking?"

Do what? Chase thought. *What did I do?*

"At least you used glue stick. They shouldn't come down with too much trouble." Her voice had grown stronger as she'd come further awake. Now she was sounding as if she were sitting next to him on the curb. "You're going to need to clean up this mess yourself. Maybe you can talk Danielle into helping you, after you apologize, but if she doesn't want to, then you need to do it yourself."

He was too afraid to ask, but God, he wished he knew what she was talking about.

"If you aren't drinking again, Chase, then you need to tell me what's going on with you. Because this is getting scary. Way too scary."

"I'm not drinking."

I'm losing my mind.

Or my life.

Or my soul.

Pick one.

"Then what's going on? What's with the pictures all over Danielle's walls?"

Pictures on Danielle's walls. That was what she was upset about. He'd used glue stick to paper her walls with pictures. Why the hell had he done that?

Write it down, Chase thought. *So you won't forget.*

"Chase?"

"What kind of pictures?"

"Pictures of Danielle. You don't remember?"

"I don't know what's going on. I'm having these little . . . *lapses*, and I forget sometimes what I've done. I don't remember doing anything to Danielle's room."

"Then you need to go see someone. A psychologist." Karla sighed heavily. "Maybe a regular doctor first, in case it's a physical problem. But either way, you need to see someone."

"I know." He could feel it coming again . . . that narrowing, when he's starting to drift away.

David B. Silva / 147

"Where are you right now?"

Chase glanced at his surroundings. On the far edge of town, where the streetlights begin to disappear and the roads get narrow. "At the bar," he said softly.

"You coming home?"

"After I close up."

And that was the last he remembered.

After that, Chase was gone.

PART IX:
EVERYTHING IN ITS TIME

1

Chase opened his eyes and there was nothing but blue.

Soft, powdery blue.

He was on his back, his hands cupped behind his head, and there was the sound of the wind through the trees. Leaves rustling. Calmness. Leaves rustling. Calmness. The air cool and refreshing. The sky, the powdery blue sky, so incredibly peaceful. This was heaven. Or if it wasn't heaven, it was what heaven should be.

There was a salty fragrance in the air.

There was dirt compressed between his toes.

No, not dirt . . . mud.

No . . . *sand.*

Chase sat up. This wasn't what he'd imagined. He wasn't in the mountains; he was on the beach. The sound of the wind through the trees? That was actually the sound of waves breaking over the shoreline.

He was on the coast.

What? A hundred and fifty miles from home?

He looked up the beach and spotted his car parked at the top of a dune, next to a garbage can, a public restroom, and a few other cars. In the far distance, he could see two people walking along the shoreline, a couple with a dog running ahead of them. Not far off shore, a flock of seagulls circled above something floating on the surface of the water. Farther out, he could see fishing boats bobbing on the surface like toys.

There was something so familiar about this place.

Chase brushed the sand off his hands, and climbed to his feet. He picked up his shoes and socks, and carried them with him as he walked along the beach, in the direction of what appeared to be a wharf in the distance.

Wind blew in his face.

Water splashed over his feet.

The ocean churned and ebbed, churned and ebbed.

God, when was the last time he had felt like this? Felt *alive* like this?

He combed a hand through his hair, and shaded his eyes—even with the sunglasses the reflection off the white sand was nearly blinding—taking in as much of the scenery as he could absorb. The driftwood scattered about, smooth and round. Seaweed that had washed ashore. A dead fish that had decomposed to the point where it was unrecognizable, though the stench lingered and was nearly intolerable.

He'd been right. That dark line in the distance was a wharf. It looked familiar, and as Chase approached, it seemed even more familiar, though he couldn't put a finger on the reason why. It wasn't so familiar he felt he'd been here before.

The shoreline went from hot sand, to pebbles, to rocks. The ocean changed its song as the waves broke against the pilings. Chase climbed an embankment up to the wharf, where people strolled casually along the wood plank corridor. Grandma's Gifts stood off to the right, the picture window in the front decorated with starfish and netting.

And there's a candy store farther up, Chase thought. *Selling salt water taffy.*

And a place that gives boat rides around the bay.

And a restaurant called The Lighthouse.

It was coming back to him now. This was a familiar

All the Lonely People / 152

place. This was the town where he'd been born. He'd spent his first nine years here. How in the hell . . .

Chase bumped into a woman dressed in a thick ski jacket and reading a book. She looked up at him, smiled politely and they both apologized simultaneously. As she continued down the wharf, Chase watched her awhile, thinking how nice her smile was, and how it reminded him of someone else.

He leaned against the railing and gazed out across the ocean, watching the silver sun dance across the waves, feeling connected for the moment. Feeling solid. Whole.

Then he closed his eyes . . .

2

And woke up sitting in a bar.

Gradually, Chase became oriented to his new surroundings. The booth was situated in a corner at the back, where the lighting was dim and the smell of urine strong. Immediately to his left, stood a door with a sign that read: Restrooms. That explained the smell.

The table top was resin-covered pine with more nicks than he'd care to count, and a spot in the corner where someone had written the initials L.G.B. in black felt-tip pen. The floor was cheap linoleum, a brown-and-white fake-tile pattern that was curling around the edges.

On the table in front of him, sat a glass of beer, the bubbles no longer rising, but the frothy head still thick. He hadn't been sitting here long, assuming this was his first drink.

The door to the restrooms opened. Chase looked up as a man who was easily 300 pounds stepped out, blindly fumbling with the belt beneath his huge belly. He nodded, and grinned wide enough to display a missing front tooth.

"That should keep me for another hour or two," he said heartily. He shuffled along the narrow corridor, back to the counter, where he settled on a stool that vanished as soon as he sat down.

This was not a familiar place.

All the Lonely People / 154

Not even vaguely familiar.

Through a window at the far end of the room, darkness peered in, disrupted by the headlights of an occasional passing car. The group of men at the bar, and one woman stuck in the middle, were all focused on a television mounted near the ceiling. There was a football game on. From where he was sitting, Chase couldn't tell who was playing and it didn't matter. What did matter was that a night game usually meant Sunday or Monday, so now he had a rough idea of the day of the week.

He looked at the beer again.

The froth had nearly disappeared. A drop of condensation trailed down one side.

There was no way to be absolutely sure, but Chase didn't think he'd taken a sip. The glass was nearly full, and he imagined that one sip would have quickly led to another, and he would have emptied the glass in record time. So that was the good news . . . he probably hadn't started down that road. The bad news was that he'd brought himself to a point where all it would take was a sip, and he had done it while being completely unaware of himself.

So now what?

He turned the glass slowly, mesmerized by the golden color. His mouth was dry, his bones cold.

One sip wouldn't hurt.

One little sip.

Chase raised the glass . . .

David B. Silva / 155

3

And it was dark.

Chase felt as if he were absorbed by the darkness, part of it. He raised his hand in front of him, turned it over, and couldn't see even the faintest hint of its outline.

He was sitting, not standing. When he tried to adjust his position, he realized this wasn't the hard surface of the bench he'd been sitting on at the bar. This seat was soft and contoured. There was an armrest on his right, made of hard plastic, and on his left . . . a door.

He was sitting in the car.

Out in the middle of nowhere again. In the middle of the night.

Except there were no stars overhead, no horizon cut into the distant sky.

This was complete darkness.

Chase found the door handle, raised it and pushed the door open. Immediately, the dome light went on and the warning beep sounded. The keys were in the ignition. That was okay. Even the warning, as incessant and irritating as he usually found it, was okay. At least he was in familiar territory. At least he was still alive.

The dome light did little to illuminate the surroundings, so Chase fumbled around on the dash board until he found the knob for the headlights. When he gave it a tug, the entire area exploded in light. He

All the Lonely People / 156

shaded his eyes, did his best to look beneath the light, and realized the car was sitting in the middle of the garage.

He was home.

Chase nearly broke out laughing.

He was home!

How long had it been?

The first thing he wanted was to visit Danielle's room and make sure she was all right. Then he'd check on Karla—make sure she was doing well, too—and jump into the shower. He couldn't remember the last time he'd taken a shower. He was long past the point of feeling dirty, and he could barely stand the smell of his own body.

Chase leaned into the car to grab the keys out of the ignition. When he couldn't pull them free, he sat back down, and his eyes were drawn to the passenger seat. All at once, the breath went out of his lungs.

Sitting in the seat was a black figure. It appeared almost human, remarkably thin, with ragged holes here and there where it looked as if acid had eaten through the very fabric of its existence.

A *straggler*.

Chase had no idea where he'd come up with that name. All he knew was that this thing sitting in the passenger seat had a name and it was *straggler*. He also knew, without knowing how, that it had been hovering around the edge of his perception for some time now. There were some things he didn't know, however. He didn't know why he could suddenly see it, and he didn't know what it wanted.

The *straggler* turned in his direction, its facial features barely discernible against the mask of writhing gloom. There was a vague impression of a mouth and nose, and eyes that were bright glowing spheres of orange.

Chase felt his body turn numb. His fingers were frozen around the keys, which were still embedded in the ignition switch. His other hand hovered above the release button on the other side of the steering wheel. The

David B. Silva / 157

warning chime he'd found so comforting just moments ago was now slowly driving him mad.

He pressed down on the release button.

The *straggler* didn't move.

Chase pulled the key free from the ignition.

The warning sound fell silent.

In his mind, he'd assumed the headlights would go off, too. That would have given him a moment of surprise, a moment when he could jump out of the car, slam the door, and head for the house. But the headlights didn't go off, and Chase found himself back to where he'd started: his body numb and unwilling to move, the *straggler* within arm's length, and . . .

Chase felt a familiar tug and realized it was coming again . . . another *lapse*.

Not now! Please, not now!

Its eyes blazing, the *straggler* opened its maw, which kept expanding until it appeared bigger than its head had been. A sour, putrid odor escaped. It moaned, a horrid mournful sound that seemed to last forever, and began to move over the armrest separating them.

Chase fell backward, out of the car, landing hard on the concrete floor.

The *straggler* followed, and . . .

All the Lonely People / 158

4

Chase opened his eyes in broad daylight.

He was sitting in the car again, a place that had apparently become his new home.

The car was parked in a lot, outside a Wal-Mart. There were two little girls, both around five or six, staring in at him through the windshield. They giggled and went running to catch up with their mother who had gone ahead in search of a cart.

There was an offensive, decayed odor all around him. Chase rolled down the windows and let the cool breeze sweep through. He closed his eyes briefly, feeling tired and disoriented. But then he'd been feeling tired and disoriented all the time lately. He should be getting used to it.

The Post-It note was on the dashboard, over the radio, not just stuck there but also Scotch taped. There were other notes. One read: *You grew up in Monterey. Don't forget the wharf.* Another read: *You haven't started drinking again. Keep it that way.* And another: *The straggler's after you.*

The straggler, Chase thought. That sounded bad.

There was another note on the dashboard. This one seemed different from the others. It wasn't a warning; it was a request. It read: *Call Ben Tucker.*

It didn't happen to say who Ben Tucker was or why he

was supposed to call him, but Chase didn't let that bother him. He had to know this Tucker fellow from somewhere. And apparently it was important that he talk to him, otherwise what was the sense in writing a note?

Ben Tucker.

There was a bank of telephones sitting out front of the Wal-Mart. The one on the far end still had a telephone book attached to the cord. Chase hunted through the white pages until he found the name Tucker. There were several columns of Tuckers, but only two that stuck out. The first was a B.H. Tucker, living off Mallard Road. The second was the exact name: Ben Tucker. Chase started by calling the second name.

"Is this Ben Tucker?"

"What do you want?" The voice belonged to a man who sounded like he might be in his seventies. Weak and raspy. Not particularly pleasant. "You calling to see if I'm still alive? Well, you can call again some other time because sure enough I'm here and I'm as alive today as I ever was."

"I have a note to call you."

"Yeah? Who gave you the note?"

I gave it to myself, Chase thought. *I just don't remember when or why, or who you are exactly.*

"I don't know," he said. "It was left on my windshield."

"You've seen 'em, haven't you?"

The *stragglers.*

Chase made that connection almost instantly. Ben Tucker was talking about the *stragglers.* Which meant he'd seen them, too. "I've seen them."

"Sorry to hear that," the man said softly. "Thought I could keep 'em away, but they still come around. See 'em out of the corner of my eye most of the time. Shadows against the wall. Watching. Waiting."

"Waiting for what?"

"For me to die. If you've seen 'em yourself, they're waiting for you, too."

All the Lonely People / 160

"Do you . . . " Chase glanced up at a toothpick-of-a-man walking with his wife, who was overweight and wearing a black oversized tee-shirt that barely covered her belly. He turned away from the middle-aged couple, and spoke softer. " . . . ever lose time? You know, like when you wake up and you're somewhere else? That sort of thing?"

"I know you, don't I?"

"That's just it, see, I don't know. You sound familiar, but I don't recognize your name, and I can't remember ever meeting you."

"Yes," Ben Tucker said quietly. "I don't notice it anymore, 'cause I pulled all the clocks out of the wall, so I don't know what time it is—hell, I don't even know what day it is anymore—but yeah, I have periods when time seems to disappear."

"Do you know what's happening? What's causing it?"

There was a long silence on the other end of the line. Chase watched a young woman shepherd her son and daughter across the slow-moving traffic and into the store. He waited, afraid to hang up because this was a *connection* and it had been longer than he could imagine since he'd connected with anyone.

"Mr. Tucker?"

Continued silence.

Chase shifted from one foot to the other and leaned against the metal cubicle around the phone. Absently, he scratched at the bandage on his arm. It had been white once, but now it was a light brownish color with dark brown edges. He had no idea what was underneath the bandage, how long it had been on his arm, or why it itched.

"Mr. Tucker? Please."

Then Chase closed his eyes and drifted away.

Part X:
Family Matters

1

"Mr. Hanford?"

Chase glanced up and there was a man standing in the doorway. The man was chewing on a stick of gum with the kind of effort you usually saved until most of the flavor had already bled out. He wasn't quite as old Chase, but he was close. His red-and-gold 49ers jacket was open; there was a white dress shirt underneath.

He raised his eyebrows. "I wake you? You look like you're half asleep."

They were in the office, at the back of The Last Stop. The ceiling fan was turning clockwise, lazily circulating the heat from a floor heater next to the desk. The phone was off the hook. There were Post-It notes plastered all over the desktop, covering bills and invoices, most of the computer screen, even the empty mug sitting on the corner.

"Who are you?" Chase asked.

The man shook his head and looked like he couldn't quite believe the question. "You want to pretend you don't know me, Mr. Hanford, I'll play along, but you better understand that the clock's ticking. It's your money you're wasting, not mine."

"Just tell me your name, will you?"

"Marc Trustman. You hired me. I'm a private detective." The man stepped into the room and handed

Chase a note. "You told me to give you this if there was a problem."

The note was in Chase's handwriting, another Post-It written in black felt-tip pen. On the front side, it read: *This is Marc Trustman. You hired him to find the old man with the box.* On the back side, it finished: *The box is what's causing the time loss and attracting the stragglers.*

"You read this?" Chase asked.

"Yeah."

"It make any sense to you?"

"Not a lick."

It didn't make any sense to Chase, either. "I didn't tell you what I meant about the box?"

"All you said was that the old man carried it into your bar one night and that was when all the trouble started. Then you asked me to see if I could track down the old guy for you."

"When did this take place?"

"Three days ago. And yeah, I got an address for you." Trustman pulled out the chair on the other side of the desk and sat down. He fished around in the pocket of his jacket and came out with a small notebook, which he opened. He tore out a page and handed it to Chase. "The guy's name is Chester Dugan. He lives in Sacramento. Used to work for a business that supplies paper products to printing companies and newspapers up and down the state. Retired in 2000. Never had any kids. Lives with his wife, Stephanie."

There was a house address and a phone number, too. "How'd you find him?"

"That's what I do," Trustman said, sitting back in the chair. "I find people."

"You sure this is the guy?"

"Wouldn't be here if I wasn't."

"What about the box?"

"What about it?"

"Does he still have it?"

All the Lonely People / 166

"Best I can tell, he keeps it at the house most of the time. I saw him carry it out to the car in a cardboard box once. You would have thought it was all he had left in the world the way he placed it in the car. He tied it down with the seatbelt."

Chase read through the information Trustman had brought him a second time, trying to find a place in his memory where it all fit. He could almost picture the old man coming into the bar with the cardboard box and plopping it down on the counter. It felt real, but real the way a dream sometimes feels real. He couldn't be sure how much was real and how much was just filling in the blanks with the information Trustman had given him.

"If you don't have any other questions then, all I need is a check and I'll be on my way," Trustman said.

Absently, Chase looked up from the piece of paper. "How much I owe you?"

"The second half. $750."

"$1500 to find this guy?"

"You seemed rather desperate at the time. Said it was a matter of life or death. That's why I put everything else on hold. To hunt this guy down for you. Gotta say, though, you didn't look half as bad off then as you do now. I don't know what's going on with you, man, but you look like you need to hit the sack for a couple of days."

"I've been under some stress lately."

"Yeah, well, it looks like it's killing you."

Before he wrote out a check, Chase pulled out a blank Post-It and wrote a note to himself. It read: *Visit this guy. He has the box. The box is the key.* Chase attached the Post-It to the piece of paper from the private detective, then wrote out a check for $750 and passed it across the desk.

Marc Trustman gave the check a close inspection, then stuffed it into the pocket of his 49er jacket, and gave the pocket a pat. He stood up, still working hard on that stick of gum. "You need anything else, you just let me know."

David B. Silva / 167

"I'll do that," Chase said.

Before he left, Trustman caught himself and stopped in the doorway. "Hey, you know that thing with the notes? That's getting a little out there, man. Seriously, you might want to see someone about it. Know what I mean?"

Chase knew exactly what he meant.

And he couldn't have agreed more.

2

Herb Canfield couldn't stand it any longer.

The headphones had helped some at first. When he turned the volume up all the way, everything else was blocked out and it was as if nothing existed except the music. But that had only worked for a short time. Gradually, even Credence Clearwater Revival at full volume wasn't enough to prevent what was happening to him.

Canfield took a long draw from the bottle of Red Dog. With his head lowered, he stared across the room at the dark figures milling around the edges. The *vultures*, he called them. They were shadows against the walls, black ghosts lingering in the corners. Elusive. Formless, except for a sense of body, a sense of face that was difficult to define. Fiery eyes that watched everything.

Waiting.

Always waiting.

Enough to drive him crazy.

"Get out of here, you sick little bastards!" Canfield balanced the neck of the empty bottle in his hand and tossed it at the nearest *vulture*. The bottle shattered against the wall. Pieces rained down on the corner, covering the floor. The *vulture's* eyes narrowed, but the creature didn't move. "Leave me alone! Go find some other poor sucker to hover over!"

It had been over a week since he'd shaved, about the same since he'd last showered. Canfield scratched at the stubble on his face, then climbed out of the chair and went to the kitchen, carrying the portable Sony CD player in one hand, the headphones covering his ears. He pulled another beer out of the refrigerator, twisted off the cap and downed half the beer in a single, long draw. He wiped his face with the back of his hand and belched.

"Parasites!"

Canfield stumbled back into the living room, plopped down in the chair and closed his eyes. Sometimes it was better to pretend they weren't there. Close his eyes and he could almost lose himself to the music. Which was better than losing himself to what? The nothingness? Because that's what had begun to happen. Every day, a little more of him seemed to disappear. First, it had been a memory here and there—where he'd left the car keys, the name of the bar he stopped in every night, the last time he'd talked to his father in St. Louis—the kind of forgetfulness that came with getting older, even though he was only forty-seven. Then he'd started having trouble remembering what he'd done yesterday. Or how the mail had appeared in a neat little stack next to the phone. Or when he'd made the tuna fish sandwich that was sitting on the coffee table uneaten.

Time started to feel like it was all running together, like paint melting off a canvas.

That was the way he'd begun to feel, too.

Credence broke into "Bad Moon Rising" and Canfield pictured himself standing in the grass of a meadow, watching a dark red moon rise up over the mountaintops, bigger than the Earth, looking like a giant eyeball staring down at him. He scratched at the stubble on his face again, took another long pull from the Red Dog.

The hardest thing was admitting it to himself: he was dying. Piece by piece, he was disintegrating. His past, his memories, his reason for living . . . they had all emptied out of him and all that was left was the shell of the man he

All the Lonely People / 170

used to be.

Canfield opened his eyes again, and stared at the *vultures* around the edges.

You know you're dying. Just get it over with.

At least it would be on his own terms. At least he would go out with a semblance of dignity. The *vultures* would win, of course. But they were going to win anyway. There was no getting around them. They were here to stay, here until the end.

How?

Did it matter?

Canfield tore the headphones off his ears for the first time in longer than he could remember. The world turned instantly quiet, except for the sound of water filling the ice maker in the refrigerator and the ringing in his ears. He went from the living room to the master bathroom at the back of the house, where he dug out the remaining gel tabs from a package of over-the-counter sleep medication. He washed them down with the last of the Red Dog. From there, he went out to the garage and brought back a twenty-five foot extension cord, plus a ladder.

Following close behind, the *vultures* slid and slithered along the walls.

"Keep up, you sick little blood suckers," Canfield said. "You don't want to miss this."

There was a trap door set in the ceiling of the hall that opened into the attic where the central heater was mounted. With the extension cord over one shoulder, he climbed the ladder, popped the door open and clumsily maneuvered his way into the crawl space. He wrapped one end of the cord around the center brace of a truss, tied it off, and tossed the excess down the hole, where it rode down the ladder and unwound on the hall floor.

Chase followed it down.

There had to be no backing out, no way to change his mind.

For that to happen, he needed some extra courage.

He returned to the kitchen, pulled another Red Dog out of the refrigerator and downed it in a few long swigs, watching the *vultures* over the bottle. They had a sense of what was going on. They were gathering around the edges like school kids around a fight during recess. Curious. Interested.

"Almost ready," Canfield said. He opened the refrigerator and took out another beer. "One more for the road."

When the bottle was empty, he tossed it at the nearest *vulture*. It passed through the creature with no discernible affect, and shattered against the cabinets. An explosion of glass showered the room. It sounded like a gentle wind chime, raining down on the metal stove, the tile floor.

Canfield laughed.

They had form, but no substance.

Like me, Canfield thought. *Just like me.*

Back down the hall—which he was barely able to navigate because his legs seemed to have taken on a mind of their own—he climbed the first three rungs of the ladder. He braced himself and gave the extension cord a good, honest tug to make sure it would hold. Better than rope, it seemed. Then he wrapped the cord around his neck three times, in loops that were snug without being tight.

Canfield buried his head in his hands.

How had he come to this point? All those years . . . put them together and they made up a lifetime. What a waste. He lived alone, which meant he'd probably never been married. Probably never had kids. Doubted he'd ever accomplished anything at work. He had existed. That was all, just *existed*. A rung or two up from the cow in the pasture who chews its cud all day. Hell, even the damn cow contributed meat to the world. What had he ever contributed?

The *vultures* collected at both ends of the hall, in the corners like spiders who think you can't see them because

All the Lonely People / 172

they aren't moving. But Canfield could see them. He could see them all.

"Parasites! Can't wait, can you?"

He stood on the ladder, two feet off the ground, scared beyond belief. But this had been coming on for a long time, he imagined, and when your memories were gone, your hopes, there wasn't anything left worth living for anyway.

"See you guys in hell," Canfield said.

Then he stepped off the ladder.

3

Chase had vanished.

That was the long and short of it. He hadn't been home in days. Hadn't called since that night they came home from the hospital and found Danielle's room plastered with her pictures. He wasn't answering his cell phone. Worse of all, he hadn't opened The Last Stop for several days.

Karla knew that because she'd grown tired of calling the bar and getting no answer, so she'd gone down to check in case something had happened and he couldn't get to the phone. When she realized Chase's car wasn't parked in the lot, front or back, she'd left without going in to look around. Wasn't much reason to bother, she figured.

But Chase was still missing, and that had become reason enough.

She sat in the car, which was parked just outside the entrance to The Last Stop. It had been several years since she'd been here. Time had a way of slipping by when you weren't paying attention, and all of Karla's attention had been focused on Danielle.

She turned the radio off, and got out of the car with the ring of keys (the one with the nail file and toe clippers in case anyone ever attacked) jingling in her hand. It took several attempts to get the door unlocked. She'd

All the Lonely People / 174

forgotten what the key looked like and it became a matter of trial and error before she found the right one. Once the door swung open, Karla dropped the keys back in her purse and went through.

The interior hadn't changed in twenty years. There was the jukebox next to the door, the booths to the left, restrooms at the back near the office, the old boat oar tacked to the wall. Before she entered, she could have closed her eyes and given a complete description of the place without missing a single detail. Except . . .

Except for the Post-It notes.

The walls were covered with them. Hundreds. Thousands. A rainbow of colors and sizes.

The air went out of Karla's lungs. She fell back against the door. *My God, Chase, what's going on with you?*

It was as if she'd stepped inside her husband's head. She turned to the notes on the wall beside her, and read down the list, one after the other.

Call Marc Trustman and see what he's come up with: the old man and the box.

You need to pay PG&E before the 25th.

Maddie Ashburn's at the YWCA. She's just like you.

You keep the key to the safe taped under the middle drawer of the desk.

If you're here, you probably don't need to be. No one comes here anymore.

Not all the notes were dated, but those that were seemed to demonstrate a gradual disintegration in Chase's handwriting. Some were clear and concise and easy to read. Others were scrawled at a slant, with some letters large, others microscopic, and all of them nearly impossible to decipher.

What had he meant when he wrote: *She's just like you?*

She read the notes adhered to the jukebox next, then those covering the front window, then the wall beyond that, around the corner. Most were minor in nature, the kind of notes you might write to remind yourself what to

David B. Silva / 175

pick up at the grocery store on the way home after work. But others were more . . . disturbing.

The one that stunned her, really stunned her, read: *You're married to Karla. And you have a daughter by the name of Danielle. They're the only people in the world who care about you.*

Karla pulled that one off the wall. She sat down at the nearest booth, head in hand, and read it over several times.

My God, Chase, what's happening to you?

4

The house was a modest track home in a suburb of Sacramento. It had a small front yard with a white-rock border around a healthy, well-kept lawn. There was a flower garden across the front, beneath the huge picture window that looked out from the living room, and a ceramic wind chime that hung from a beam over the entrance.

A gentle drizzle was falling.

It wasn't cold out, but it wasn't warm, either.

This was the house of the old man. The old man had the box. The box had something to do with the way his time had been evaporating and his memories had disappeared. That was the story as Chase understood it, stripped down to its bare essentials because that was all he had left . . . just the bare essentials, written in long hand on a scattering of notes.

Chase went over his notes one more time, made sure he remembered everything that had been given to him about the old man, then climbed out of the car and went to the front door. On the doorstep, he felt around in his jacket pocket to make sure he still had his notepad and his pen. Once he confirmed they were with him, he knocked on the door.

It was answered by a woman in her late sixties, with a warm smile and bright hazel eyes. When she didn't recognize him, she asked, "May I help you?"

"Stephanie Dugan?"

"Yes."

"I was wondering if I could speak with your husband?"

"Chester? I'm sorry, he's out of town."

"Do you know when he'll be returning?"

"Not for a few days, I'm afraid." Stephanie Dugan was cautious enough to keep her hand on the door and her body blocking the doorway, but she wasn't afraid. A different generation, Chase imagined. When you didn't have to worry about who came to your door. "Is there something I can help you with?"

"I worked with Chester, before he retired."

"Oh, I'm so sorry he's going to miss you. I'm sure he would have loved to have talked over old times."

"Is there any way I might be able to meet up with him?"

"I'm sorry."

"Mrs. Dugan . . . please. As I'm sure you can tell, I'm not in the best of health. Time is running out for me. If at all possible, I really do need to see your husband."

She wasn't impolite about it, but she gave him a thorough looking over. Chase could only imagine how bad he looked. He hadn't shaved or showered in days. His clothes were dirty. He'd lost weight. There were dark circles under his eyes from a lack of sleep. If their roles had been reversed, he would have closed the door and probably felt safer doing so.

"I didn't catch your name," she said.

"Chase Hanford."

"All right, Mr. Hanford. I'll see what I can do." She stepped back and opened the door to him. "If you'd like to come in and sit down while I check for you."

"Thank you."

She directed him to a chair in the living room, then excused herself while she went to get some papers. This was a room for show, Chase imagined. People rarely

All the Lonely People / **178**

spent time here. The walls were beige, the carpet a bright virgin white, the sofa and chair off white. There was a wall of photographs, next to a stone fireplace that used natural gas, and a marble-top coffee table with recent issues of *Newsweek, Readers Digest,* and *Vanity Fair.*

Chase poked around a bit, until he found himself standing in front of the wall of photographs. There was an 8x10 of the two of them sitting cheek-to-cheek on a cruise ship. A wedding picture. A formal family portrait, taken when they were in their forties, with brothers and sisters, everyone appearing about the same age, everyone with a smile. A backyard barbecue with Stephanie looking up from a picnic table. Her face was gaunt, eyes dark, complexion ghostly. She was wearing a turban over her head.

"That was in the middle of my chemo."

Chase glanced up to find Mrs. Dugan standing in the doorway.

"It's not very flattering, I'm afraid, but it reminds me how every day is a precious gift."

Chase nodded. It was a lesson he'd just recently begun to learn himself.

"I'm sorry I can't tell you exactly where Chester is at the moment; he's been doing some contract work for a company that keeps him traveling up and down the state. He calls nearly every night, though, and he was in Red Bluff last night." She sat down on the sofa and unfolded a California map. "I think he said something about staying in Corning tonight."

Corning was only a couple hours away.

Chase took out his notebook and wrote down: *the old man, the box, in Corning tonight.*

"Do you know what day this is?"

"Wednesday."

Chase added the day, and he apologized for all the notes, explaining he'd been having trouble with his memory lately. He never said anything about why his memory was failing, or what was going on in his life that made speaking to her husband so urgent, and she didn't ask. Chase had the impression that she thought he was going through something similar to what she had gone through. Sometimes they ravished your mind as well as your body.

Mrs. Dugan pointed out where Corning was on the map, showed him the route along I-5, which was probably the quickest way to get there, though it wasn't the shortest. She showed him another route along 99w, which was closer to a straight line, but went for long stretches with only two lanes. Your choice, she said. It was six-of-one, half dozen of the other. Then she asked if she could make a sandwich or a snack for him to take with him.

Chase liked her. He liked her a lot. She was a kind-hearted woman.

He passed on the food, however, explaining that he was eager to get going. She said she understood, and showed him to the door.

"Thanks for all your help," Chase said.

"You're welcome. Tell Chester I love him."

"I will."

It was early afternoon.

All the Lonely People / 180

PART XI:
IT'S ALL RIGHT, MA, I'M ONLY DYING

1

Corning was a small town, population of around 7,000. It had the feel of most mid-California small towns . . . hot in the summer, comfortable in the winter, a farming community at heart, trying to hold onto its heritage but gradually succumbing to the car dealerships and fast food restaurants. It would always be known as The Olive City. No need for explanation.

Chase came into town on 99w, past an old water tower that stood next to the highway. The drizzle had followed him all the way up the state, keeping the sky dark until evening turned to night and lights began to go on at the farm houses, then the businesses.

He stopped at B & B's Crossroads first. No one there had ever head of a Chester Dugan. They suggested he try up the road at the Green Doors Tavern, but Chase had no success there, either.

It was half-past six and the other side of town when he stopped by a place called The Watering Hole. The old man was sitting at the bar, his back to Chase, but it was him all right. The image of him with his wife in the photographs on the wall back in Sacramento were still fresh in Chase's mind. Dugan was shorter than he'd imagined, hunched forward, a single beer on the counter in front of him, and next to that . . . the box.

There was a crowd gathered around.

Chase came up from behind and peered over the

David B. Silva / 183

shoulder of a man in a red plaid shirt.

"It's called a spirit box," Dugan said. He went into his story about the box being a gift you gave to your enemy, and how it captured the enemy's soul.

Chase wiggled and worked his way in closer.

"Open it!" someone shouted from the back.

"Yeah, open it!"

Dugan looked across the counter at the bartender. "Would you mind? Would it be okay?"

"Don't matter to me none."

"It matters to me," Chase said. He clamped his hand down on Dugan's forearm and moved it away from the box. "I think you and I have something to talk about."

"Do I know you?"

"The Last Stop. Remember?"

Dugan's face brightened. Not what Chase had expected. "Yes, yes. I do. I remember. You were the gentleman behind the bar. The owner of the place. How on earth did you ever find me?"

"I stopped by your home in Sacramento. Your wife put me on to you."

The brightness in the old man's face turned instantly white. "Is she—?"

"She's fine. I didn't hurt her. But we need to talk."

All the Lonely People / 184

2

Dugan didn't want to talk in the parking lot, so Chase followed him in the car to a Burger King, where they sat down across from each other over coffee. Dugan placed the box in the seat beside him, against the wall as if he were making sure no one could steal it.

"You look like hell," he said.

"Gee, I wonder why?"

"I'm surprised you're still alive."

"I think it's because I didn't stare at the light."

"Really?"

"Just a guess," Chase said. "You'd know better than me."

"I don't know that much about it, to be honest. Just the basics."

"Where did you get it?"

"A stranger brought it to me." Dugan took a sip of his coffee, and kept his hands wrapped around the cup for warmth. It always felt cold in Burger King in the winter. "It was when Steph was at her worst. We didn't know if she was going to make it or not. The treatments were hard on her and the doctors weren't saying anything hopeful. I was growing more and more desperate everyday. Then this guy corners me outside Steph's room one day. He says he has something that could help. Well, those were words I hadn't heard before, not in a long, long time. I would have followed him down a collapsing mine shaft if he could help my wife get better."

"Where did he get the box?"

"I didn't ask."

"Why did he give it to you?"

Dugan, who looked haggard—his face long, the color dark, eyes dull—stared off to the distance in thought. "I think he'd come to the same place, I've come. It had turned into a burden. The only way out was to pass it to someone new."

Chase bowed his head slightly, feeling the exhaustion catching up with him again. He nodded, then forced himself to focus. "At the bar, when you opened it, what happened exactly? What did it do to everyone?"

"Let me show you." Dugan removed the box from its cardboard container and placed it on the table. "Give me your hand."

Chase didn't move. He didn't know what would happen when the box was opened, that was a note that he'd never written to himself, but he knew nothing good could come from it. "Why? What are you going to do?"

"Put your hand on the box and the light can't hurt you. As long as you're touching it, you're part of it."

"What about everyone else here?"

"We'll move." Dugan stood up with the box under his arm. "To the back, where no one will be bothered. It'll be fine. The light only covers a few feet. No one will be harmed. Trust me."

At the back of the room, Dugan placed his hand flat against the side of the box. He asked Chase to do the same. Then he raised the lid. The area exploded in a bright white light. It was nearly blinding in its intensity. Chase shaded his eyes with his left hand. He'd seen this light before. It was coming back to him now, that night in the bar, with everyone gathered around to see what was in the box.

"Look inside," Dugan said. "You didn't see this

All the Lonely People / 186

before. Some of your friends no doubt did, but you missed it."

Chase leaned forward and gazed down into the box. At the bottom, there was a mass of writhing creatures, grayish in the light, pawing and mewing. They looked like naked rats, only without the tails. Their mouths were open, their eyes closed.

"You're in there," Dugan said solemnly. "Your friends from the bar are in there. You're all in a state of transition. When one of you dies, his energy becomes Steph's energy. You see? That's how she was able to recover from her cancer. That's how she's stayed alive."

"Why us? Why The Last Stop?"

"Because you were already dead."

"You didn't even know us."

"I knew your kind. I used to be one of you. Going through the motions everyday. No real connections with family or friends. You'd already made your pact with death. You were fully prepared to go whenever the time came. In your mind, there was nothing else to live for."

Chase hated to admit it, but he was right.

Dugan closed the lid. "You can remove your hand now."

"Am I going to die?"

"Yes."

"How soon?"

"Everyone's a little different."

Chase closed his eyes. The pain caused by the light felt as if it were seeping deep into his brain. There was a part of him that wanted it to be over right now, this moment. He was tired of not remembering, of losing chunks of time when he didn't know where he'd been or what he'd been doing. It would be so much easier if he could close his eyes and simply fade away.

"There's a way out if you want it," Dugan said. "A couple ways."

That brought Chase back to the moment. "Like what?"

David B. Silva / 187

"I can pass the box to you, the way my predecessor passed it to me."

"Which means?"

"You could do one of two things. You could destroy it, which would set you and your friends free. It would also bring about the death of my wife."

"What about your death?"

Dugan looked like he was going to laugh, but he didn't. Instead, he smiled sadly. "I suppose that would be a nice little bonus in your eyes. Yes, it would mean my death, too."

"What's the alternative?"

"You could carry on, use the box to lengthen the life of someone you know."

Like Danielle, Chase thought. She had cystic fibrosis, according to the notes he'd written. A life expectancy of maybe thirty if she were lucky. That hardly seemed fair. Dugan and his wife had had their share of years. Didn't Danielle deserve hers?

"But it would mean taking the energy of others."

Chase felt his eyes growing heavy. He thought of The Last Stop and the people who must have been there that night. There had to be another way. Maybe if he took the box into a hospital, where someone was on life support with no hope of recovery? Or into a convalescent home? Or a mental ward with the worst of the worst. Maybe if he only used it on the elderly? Or people dying of cancer or AIDS? Maybe on people who were already hopeless . . . drug addicts, prostitutes, convicted felons?

"Scary, isn't it?"

Chase shook himself out of the reverie. "Huh?"

"You were thinking about who might be *appropriate* if you decided to keep the box. Scary how easy it is to start adding groups to the list, isn't it?"

"What if *you* destroyed the box?"

"We'd all die."

Chase yawned. He didn't think he was going to last much longer. He downed the last of his coffee in the hope

***All the Lonely People* / 188**

that it might keep him going. "No matter what I decide to do . . . "

"There's no easy way out," Dugan said.

"Maybe if I . . . or you . . . you know . . . maybe if . . . " Chase closed his eyes and faded away.

3

Nothing had changed.

That was the first thing Chase told himself when he came out of the *lapse*.

He was sitting in the lot of a Burger King, the only car left. The windshield was coated with rain drops. There was no one else around. The security lights were on inside the building, the only lights within view. Apparently, he'd been gone for hours. Nothing new there. Next to him on the front passenger seat, was the box with a note attached.

Maybe something had changed.

Chase remembered his conversation with the old man, Chester . . . Chester Dugan. He remembered what the man had looked like, how Chase had found him, what he'd said about the box. He remembered all that. It was perfectly clear in his mind, as if it had happened just moments ago.

An incredible sense of relief washed over him. He rolled down the window, felt the cool fresh air against his face, and screamed at the top of his lungs. "I remember! I remember!"

The drizzle that had followed him all day—he remembered it following him up 99w as if there were a cloud directly over the car—had stopped now, but the air felt damp and Chase basked in all its glory for a moment.

All the Lonely People / 190

It was too soon to be certain that he was whole again, of course. But he felt alive for the first time in better than a week. His thoughts were clear. The cloud had lifted. He knew where he was and how he'd gotten here.

With the window left open, Chase leaned across the seat and peeled the note off the top of the box. It was from Dugan. As much as he could remember from their conversation, he didn't recall making any agreement about the box one way or the other. So he was surprised to find it sitting in the car with him.

The note read: *I see you enjoy writing notes to yourself. Hope this one doesn't get lost in the clutter. I've left the box in your possession, Mr. Hanford. Your memories should return. You'll still lose time here and there for awhile, as you did in the middle of our conversation, but eventually that will pass, too. You can destroy the box if you wish, or use it for your own purposes. The choice is yours. Or if you prefer, you can still return it. I'm not going to be doing any traveling for awhile. I'm going to go home and spend some time with Steph. Best of luck, whatever you choose to do. My sincere apologies for the hell I've put you through.*

The bottom was signed by Chester Dugan.

It had been hell, Chase thought. *Pure hell.*

He read through the note a second time, to make sure he hadn't missed anything. It sounded like the box was his if he wanted it. He could do with it as he pleased. There was no *easy* out, as Dugan had said—the thought of that brought a smile to Chase; he'd never realized how nice it was to remember the little things—but at least there was an out.

Even so, his initial impulse was to lay the box down in the parking lot and drive over it a couple of times. That would be the end of the road for Chester Dugan and his wife, but hell, they didn't deserve to go on after what they'd done anyway. At least the old man didn't. Chase wasn't sure if the man's wife had a clue or not about what her husband had been up to.

David B. Silva / 191

That initial impulse passed without him destroying the box, and that felt like a good thing as he started up the engine.

The cool night air had grown cold. He rolled up the window as it began to drizzle again. He turned the radio on, played around with the dial, and finally found an oldies station playing "Instant Karma" by John Lennon.

Time to go home again.

4

It was nearing four o'clock in the morning by the time he arrived.

The house was dark, except for a single light on the second floor. The master bedroom. Karla was still up.

Chase parked in the driveway, got out, and went around to the passenger side to get the box. He'd had plenty of driving time to think about what he wanted to do, and he'd come to a decision that seemed inevitable when he looked back on it. Right at the moment, however, he put that out of his mind and paused to look up at the light in the window. Why would Karla still be up at this time of night?

Inside the house, he moved slowly from room to room, taking in all the little details that were fresh in his memory. He felt like a little kid who just realized that letters made words and words made sentences and when you put them all together they told a story. He was giddy with his ability to remember things. There was the VCR in the living room that wouldn't rewind tapes; the burn in the kitchen counter where he'd put the frying pan for just a moment while he dug a kitchen towel out of a drawer. It was all so clear to him.

At the top of the stairs, Chase crossed the hall and pushed open the door to Danielle's room. It was too dark to actually see anything except the dial of the clock radio on her nightstand. He stood there a moment, breathing in his daughter's clean, youthful smell and thinking how close he'd come to losing this. Not just the last week or so, but long before that, when he'd shut himself off from both Danielle and Karla.

The door was open to the master bedroom. A shaft of light spilled out into the hallway, and Chase stepped into it as he paused in the doorway. Karla was sitting in a chair next to the bed, buried beneath an electric blanket. There was an open book in her lap, spine up. Her eyes were closed, her head bowed. She looked like an angel, caught in the light of the nightstand lamp.

His eyes drifted from Karla to the bed, where Danielle was tossing uneasily.

Even from across the room, he could see she wasn't well. There was almost no color in her lips. A sheen of sweat covered her forehead, reflecting the light. When she took in a breath it was labored and phlegmy.

Chase kneeled next to Karla and gently shook her.

Her eyes opened, dull at first, then suddenly bright with surprise. She opened her mouth to say something, but Chase put a finger across his lips to shush her.

"Downstairs," he whispered.

The moment they were out of the room, Karla whispered, "Where have you been? I've been looking all over for you."

"It's been a nightmare, but it's over now."

Downstairs in the kitchen, Karla pulled a chair out for him. "I'll make some coffee."

"That would be nice." Chase sat down. He placed the box on the table next to him, and watched her closely. He could imagine the fragrance of the Pantene shampoo in her hair, the fluffy softness of her terrycloth robe. Almost as if he were experiencing them for the first time.

"I went by The Last Stop, looking for you," Karla said, pulling a bag of coffee beans down from the cabinet. "The walls . . . every square inch was covered with your notes. It scared me, Chase. Really scared me. Especially after

All the Lonely People / 194

what you'd done to Danielle's room. I worried that maybe you'd had some sort of breakdown."

Danielle's room. That had happened during a *lapse.* He remembered waking up and finding the photographs on her walls. There had been a glue stick in his hand, and photo albums, strips of negatives and pictures scattered all over the floor. It might have looked like madness, but it wasn't. It was the only way he could keep himself from forgetting her.

Karla paused and glanced over her shoulder. "It wasn't, was it?"

"A breakdown? It was pretty close. Closer than I ever want to come again."

"You going to tell me about it?"

"You want to know?"

"Of course I do."

Chase nodded, and while she finished making the coffee, he told her about that first night when the old man had come into the bar, carrying the box. He told her about the light, and how everyone seemed disoriented afterward, and about how he'd had trouble sleeping after that.

"I remember that first night," Karla said. "You were tossing and turning and having a terrible time. You ended up going downstairs to sleep."

He told her about his eyes becoming sensitive to the light, to which Karla commented, "That's what's missing. You aren't wearing those godawful sunglasses." And about how he would wake up sometimes hours later in a strange place with no idea how he got there. And about the private detective he'd hired without remembering, and meeting the old man's wife, then the old man himself. And about the box.

"So that's the box?" Karla asked, referring to the box he'd brought with him and was now sitting on the table. She handed him a cup of coffee and sat down across from him.

"That's it." Chase looked at her, searching for a way to

David B. Silva / 195

find the words for what he wanted to say. "You know why I've always pushed her away?"

"Danielle?"

"Yeah." He let out a long, cleansing breath and stared across the room at the cabinets. "I was afraid. I thought if I got too close, I wouldn't be able to stand it if she died. It scared the daylights out of me that I might lose her. And then on top of that, there was this terrible sense of guilt. When the doctors first told us it was hereditary, that our genes were the underlying cause, that nearly killed me. I could hardly face myself in the mirror in the morning."

There were tears in Karla's eyes. She smiled sadly. "Me, too. The guilt thing. That's why I've always been so protective. I think I wanted to make up for what I'd done to her. It sounds silly, saying it out loud like this, because we had no way of knowing, but I don't think I'll ever be able to get past the guilt."

Her tears suddenly turned to great, racking sobs.

Chase held her, comforted her. "Hey, it's going to be all right."

"No, it isn't. She's dying, Chase."

"What?"

"Everything's starting to go bad," Karla said, wiping at her tears with a napkin. "She's showing signs of another lung infection. The doctor's got her on antibiotics, but he's worried because she keeps losing weight. She's getting weaker, Chase. I'm taking her in tomorrow to have tests done to make sure her lungs aren't bleeding and see how her right ventricle's holding up under the stress, but I'm so afraid we're going to lose her. I'm so afraid . . . "

Karla broke into sobs again.

Chase moved her to the other chair, where he sat her down in his lap. He held her gently, rocked her, let her cry.

What else could he do?

All the Lonely People / 196

PART XII:
THE FIRST STOP

1

Chase pulled into the parking lot, around the side of the building, into the first open space. He parked, turned off the engine, and checked the first name and address on the list.

Westside Tavern.

683 West Lamp Post Road.

He placed an "X" next to the name, then dated it.

The brick building was situated at an angle on the lot, back from the road, sheltered by several old oak trees with trunks the diameter of a 50 gallon drum. Its windows were blacked out, except for neon lights hawking Miller Genuine Draft, Bud Light, and Coors. It had been raining all afternoon, into the evening, and the gutters were overflowing with water.

Chase tucked the cardboard box under his arm. He pulled the collar of his jacket up, climbed out of the car, and made a dash for the front entrance.

It took an effort to pull the heavy door open, but it closed behind him with a shudder that went through the entire building. Faces raised up from their drinks. Eyes followed Chase across the dirty black floor to the bar. He sat on the corner stool, and placed the box on the stool next to him, covering a rip in the upholstery. Then he ordered a beer.

"Quiet tonight," he said when the beer arrived.

"Always quiet here." The man was on the thin side,

only a head taller than the cash register, which sat on the counter near the middle. He was bald on top, gray on the sides, and clean shaven. There was a cowboy riding a bucking bronco on his belt buckle, which was nearly the size of one of the mugs stacked behind the bar.

"Bet you own the place, don't you?"

"Since '62."

"Done good for you?"

"Good enough, I suppose. I'm still here."

Chase nodded. He was willing to bet it was always like this . . . a sleepy little place most people didn't even know was here. Just a few regulars, shuffling in after work, whetting their whistles and killing time before time killed them.

"Nice place," Chase said.

He raised the box off the stool and placed it on the counter.

David B. Silva has written seven novels, his most recent *The Hawke Legacy*, a novel of epic horror, spanning over forty years as Aaron Hawke leaves the innocence of childhood behind to fight a recurring evil, which is due out later this year from Subterranean Press. His first short story was published in 1981. His short fiction has since appeared in *The Year's Best Horror, The Year's Best Fantasy & Horror*, and *The Best American Mystery Stories*. In 1991, he won a Bram Stoker Award for his short story, "The Calling." In 2001, he won the International Horror Award for Best Short Story Collection for *Through Shattered Glass*. He's currently at work wrapping up some short story commitments before starting his next novel. You can join his mailing list to keep up on new projects by visiting his website at www.davidbsilva.com.